FRANK TALABER

SEEDS OF ASCENSION

BOOK ONE SPIRITS AWAKENING

DEDICATION

Dedicated To The Memory Of My Son, Rory.

Wish I Could Go Back In Time

And Bring You Back.

But I Can't.

Love You and Will Always Miss You.

Dad

FRANK TALABER, WRITER BY SOUL.

A natural storyteller, whose compelling thoughts are freed from the depths of the heart and the subconscious before being poured onto the page.

Literature written beyond the realms of genre he is known to grab readers; kicking, screaming, laughing or crying and drag them into his novels.

Or as he has often said:

> *Write like your soul is on fire and*
> *the pencil is your voice screaming.*
> *You don't have to be mad to be a writer,*
> *but it sure helps.*

Writer by Soul.
Canada's Foremost Off-Beat Author
Enter the literary worlds of Frank Talaber

OTHER NOVELS

Urban Fantasy Genre

***Stillwater Runs Deep* Series**
Book One: Raven's Lament
Book Two: The Lure
Book Three: The Awakening

Urban Fantasy/Crime/Mystery/Paranormal

The Ainsworth Chronicles
Book One: The Joining
Book Two: The Mystery of Ms. Teak

Short Story Anthology Series

Volume One: What I'd Say To Buddha If I Met Him In The Pub
Volume Two: What I'd Say To Einstein If I Met Him On The Dance Floor
Volume Three: What I'd Say To Agatha Christie If I Met Her In The Knitting Club

Spiritual/ Science Fiction Genre

Seeds Of Ascension
Book One: Spirits Awakening

FOREWORD

For those of you who are new to my books, welcome! What kept you? No, seriously, thank you for buying, or obtaining somehow, my latest muse. I hope you enjoy meeting these characters and stories as much as I did writing them. Some are old friends of mine you've met before, but some are brand new. But for now, let's get this new party started, shall we?

PRELUDE

*S*tars *hung in eternity threaten to fall into each other winking in disbelief. My breath wafts its cooling warmth into the darkness as I turn to answer the call from inside.*

That beckoning voice that brought me here.

Only there are no tomorrows, no yesterdays, and one time eternal. The now.

A cry rents the stillness. It is not possible, is it?

The pad of feet issues from somewhere. No reassurance that I will leave here alive or whole or even if my spirit will be cleansed from my bones. Nicely or rendered horribly apart like from some Grade B horror movie.

So coming here was not at all wise.

Still my breath issues forth joining the clouds that skirt soundlessly by as mist curls among trees, like angelic spirits melted into smoke tendrils by this place.

Chill surges upwards as fog thickens, cooling and undulating like a snake on a river of calling.

Whatever this is that draws me here, asking of myself questions, I have that no answers to speak before it.

Denying touch, taste, sound, smell and clamping numbness to my ears, I remain open to its only way of being.

The here. The now.

Dew drips from grass, leaves, everywhere. The soft plodding of water coming home to earth. A cycle born again, returning.

Padding sounds end as I take another step forward, answering the call that beckons.

While silence answers me with its own questions.

Once again.

Roger woke in a lurch from his dreams.

He got up and walked slowly to the bathroom making sure Beth, his wife, wouldn't wake. Outside the full moon hung in abeyance, calling to him to sleep some more and continue this insane journey he began, or at least was called to perform.

Bugger that, I have to urinate first before my bladder bursts.

He closed his eyes and let his waters flow into the toilet before him.

Yeah, I know, Words from the song echoed in him, *the Orinoco Flow.*

What a Bag.

John Lennon's song added to the echoes descending away into dribbles. 'Let it be'. Let it be, let it be, let it be. Whispering words of wisdom. Let it be.

And that was where it began.

Only it won't, will it?

Let anything be, anymore?

Chapter One

Seattle, Sea Tac Airport

"The End is near! Repent sinners! Set your spirit free, join Jehovah at the right hand of God!" The man dressed in a black suit bellowed to the crowd of people, most of whom were simply trying to get either into the airport before they missed their flight, or were waiting for their rides out of this chaos.

Unfortunately, Roger had picked a spot to get out of his taxicab right next to the Jehovah's Witness and two newly-bald Hare Krishna dressed in their flowing robes, chanting in time to the rhythm of their tambourines. "Join the pure love of God. Set your spirit free." The two chanted brazenly trying to overcome the Jehovah's Witness man thumping his bible loudly exclaimed in a baritone voice, "Ignore false prophets."

The two being ex-WFC converts didn't take well to the rude preacher stealing the show beside them with his boisterous Sunday-morning-at-the-pulpit voice and began to thump their tambourines even louder.

The Jehovah man glared and raised his voice.

Roger Harrison and his new wife Beth waited while the taxi driver unloaded their luggage as all Hell broke loose. The man in black started thumping one of the Hare Krishna over the head with his bible as the other put him in a headlock shouting, "Find the love of God and yourself." Prayer beads went flying in all directions as the Jehovah man grabbed one of the tambourines and slammed one of the Hare Krishna's in the head.

Roger glanced at his watch; they didn't have much time to make their plane, let alone watch the bizarre spectacle unfolding in front of him. Already security guards were running in from all directions adding to the ensuing melee.

"Wow, don't see that every day," Beth spurted.

An older man, obviously a former love-child of the sixties according to his long hard and faded, well-worn peace-emblem tee-shirt, shoved by Roger. "Peace Bro'."

He gave Roger the two-fingered sign once common in the sixties. Roger caught the line 'If I could turn myself inside out and set my spirit free' playing from the man's headset. U2, he thought, as he managed to squeeze into the terminal building. "I've got to help my brethren fight the fascist pigs in power, the times they are a-changing." He smiled and grabbed a fallen tambourine and belted one of the guards over the head.

"Oh, that they will be if we miss our flight. They'll be changing me into the ranks of the newly divorced." He hurried his new bride inside. "Yup," he said, "you don't get to see that every day."

Set my spirit free.

Lyrics echoed in his head.

My spirit free?

The question fluttered away. *As somewhere in the mists of his mind angels fluttered wings and rain fell on delicate ferns, uncurling into the light generated by the sun overhead.*

What?

February 4th, 1971, The Moon; Fra Mauro Crater

"One small step for man... one giant leap for mankind."

The words of Neil Armstrong echoed through Edwin Mitchell's mind as he stared up at the Earth rising over the horizon, the music of 2001: A Space Odyssey playing in his head.

Earth: continents, surrounded by the deep blue of the oceans cradled in billowy arms of clouds. He tried to spot the USA and, more importantly, the location of his hometown, where his wife and kids were probably staring back up at the moon. No markings existed to distinguish one country from another, nor to distinguish democracies from communistic societies or dictatorships. Land and mountains, ocean and clouds. Just one world spinning. Odd, he'd not really expected it to be like this.

Spinning, like so many of the other dots of light shining by the untold billions amid all this magnificence and the darkness of space, without the filter of sky and atmosphere. One spec, a mote revolving in a sea of infinity, all part of the cosmos. At peace with the universe. At one with itself.

At one with the Universe; connected.

Edwin smiled. He'd never imagined it would be like this. No lines, no boundaries out here. Nothing like he'd been told, had read about in the books: light years of frozen emptiness separated by mere molecules and photons floating in vastness. This was different. Something no books, no professors could describe, and none could experience. He was only the sixth man to walk on the moon, blessed to have left Earth and view it from the outside in. Whole, suspended in the firmament of the heavens.

Tones of awe, like angels humming in reverence, filled his head. As the light of Earth flooded the plain he stood on, Ed gasped. Lights dancing, reflecting. Lights touching him as he grasped the rocks around him. Lights dancing? On the Moon?

He turned and stared into the heavens. Flashes of flares or rocket-fire, too small to be anything propelled, streaked off the moon's surface into space. Heading in the direction of Earth.

Beep.

"Ed, your vital signs are going offline. Ed, you've stopped breathing. CO levels are rising. Ed, you okay?"

"Yes, Mission Control, I'm fine. Did you register any unusual activity?"

"Nothing other than some of the seismic sensors indicating several tremors in the area."

"How many?"

He counted the streaks heading away from the moon.

"Looks like about twelve peaks in activity, just beyond the Fra Mauro crater. Are you over the top yet?"

He counted the same number of lights ascending into the dark universal sky heading towards earth. "Another couple of steps." *They aren't going to believe this back home are they?*

He took a long breath and sighed, lost in crystalline reflections as he crested the crater.

"Ed? Everything okay? Your monitors are going nuts again."

"Jeez." *No one, absolutely no one would believe this.* He didn't believe it himself. "Just admiring old Mother Earth," he lied. "It's not every day you get to see an Earthrise."

No, nothing was as he'd been taught. Oh, it was all there, the stars, the sun, the blackness of space, everything where it should be. Only it was different, as different as the plateau before him. A whole lifetime of teachings and beliefs blown aside by invisible winds, like dust before reality's vision. He shook his head, scrambled back down the way he'd come and returned to his work of digging up moon rocks to take home. Was it possible? *Did I just see that?*

Home, he thought, how funny. In some ways as he stared up into the heavens, he was home.

Sea Tac Airport

"If I could turn myself inside out and break my spirit free."

The U2 song line stuck, stewing away in his head, too many times to be coincidence. Spinning at the unconscious like a dog digging aimlessly in the dirt at something tantalizing it smelled. Compelling him on and on.

Compelling him on and on.

The near riot outside began to die down, with the security guards resorting to Tasering and handcuffing the troublemakers. The Jehovah man yelling obscenities at the bleeding Hari Krishna's as they cursed back in some Indian dialect that only Buddha would know.

Words, all words pulling at him, like spirit things. Echoing, so strange. His whole day had begun to have a feeling of surrealism. The scene outside didn't help. He was supposed to be on his honeymoon. Buddha, incense and mystical music echoed in his head.

Echoing winds, words.

Spirit.

Drifting, pulling him away.

Intangible presences.

Pooling like dew on grass, drip, dripping, flowing into a burbling stream.

Consciousness.

Spirit flowing.

To places, dimensions unknown.

Inevitable things.

His subconscious nagging at him, it's sublime finger jabbing into his head, Roger shuffled forward joining the long queue in the ticket line.

Why? Why here? Why now?

"What are you so nervous about?" Beth prodded him.

"Who says I'm nervous?" She broke him away from his musing as fairies folded their arms and tapped their slippered feet, waiting for an answer only they knew would come.

"Because you always turn pale and squeeze your hands together, or mine."

He yanked himself back to earth and realized he'd been gripping her hand so tight her wedding band had marked her finger. "Sorry." All day he'd felt odd, like something wasn't right. That commotion outside hadn't helped ease his fears. The repeated chanting of voices? Haunting his memory like niggling tendrils of spirit things. *Fuck, get out of my head,* he swore to himself. *And where the eff did this come from? It was like what I just saw or heard twigged some memory of myself, or at least of what I once was?*

Roger simply looked blanked at his new wife, not sure what to say to mollify her, when his heart was beginning to race on a journey he'd never taken, but knew he was on. Once before.

"I don't get it. You've flown dozens of times on business. Or are you afraid of me? Don't worry I don't bite; although I do nibble rather fine. Remember the first time we kissed? I thought you were going to crush my fingers."

"And the second and the third. You know I get nervous around women." *Yes, talk to Beth, it helped to get the visions of angels out of my head. Only why are they there in the first place? He aimlessly scratched at an itchy part of his stomach that had begun to throb. Heat spread as he scratched at it.*

"Hey, I'm your wife now. It's okay."

"I know. I think lunch didn't agree with me, damn Burritos." He hugged her. A strange day threatened, that's what it was. Be prepared for the most unexpected on those days, a colleague once told him. *Easier said than done.* It reminded him of a poster from his younger days, 'It's hard to remember your objective is to drain the swamp, when you're up to your armpits in alligators.'

Roger frowned, the soft cry of a child caught his ears from somewhere in the distance or from inside his heart. "Do you hear that?" He cranked his head around, scanning the crowd.

"No, I don't. Hear what?"

"Young girl, crying." Roger spotted the young black girl standing by the candy counter about thirty feet away. No one seemed to be paying any attention to her. Everyone too busy rushing around trying to catch planes. He muttered. She was clutching a doll, tears streaming down her ebony face. "Keep our place, I'll be right back."

"You okay young lady," he bent over and held out a Kleenex as he approached.

"Can't find my mommy." She started to cry harder.

"It's okay, we'll find her. Let's go over here to security and I'll buy you a candy bar while we page her." He was careful not to touch her as they walked over to the counter. Even acts of kindness he knew could be wrongly construed. Best to be careful, didn't want to be thrown in the clink on child molestation charges on his honeymoon.

A minute later, after the pager called out the lady's name and the young girl had nearly finished the Mars bar he bought, a rather frightened large black lady came running from across the crowded terminal. "My baby! One second she was by my side and the next she was gone." She sobbed as she clutched the young girl. "Thank you, kind sir, and you young lady are going to get a good scolding."

"No problem, but be kind, she was only a child, doing what kids do, exploring strange environs."

She looked weirdly at him and crushed her kid closer to him, like he was someone suddenly not to be trusted.

He walked back to join Beth in their lineup, which had moved only about three people closer to the front. He scratched at the throb in his stomach. The heat pulsating.

"You're always helping kids. Why is that?"

"Don't know. Something to do with having no dad as I grew up. Perhaps." In his head the words, *teachers call out to those that need attention and protection before their time is ready to begin their teachings. Protectors insure the lives of the innocent so that they can one day replace them.* Echoed like an opera in the void. Why do I get the feeling this trip is nowhere where I think it will take me?

He smiled to her as the vision of some Buddhaistic being winked back at him.

"Only your mom to raise you. Must have brought out your feminine, sensitive side. Another reason why I love you. I've never met a man with such a spiritual deepness." She winked. "Just wait until I get you alone."

"Is that a promise?" *Spiritual deepness? Never had anyone say that to me before. Doesn't everyone listen to Enya in their car or Delirium?* He thought a moment as the throb in his stomach increased.

Promises, promises of inevitable things. Inevitable things unfolding. Fuck.

They were on their honeymoon, full of excitement for the new journey together as man and wife. But inside Roger sensed another journey unfolding, one he had dreamt about for days now in his dreams. Unsettling dreams, that at first he'd put it down to his anticipation of getting married, his nervousness regarding the honeymoon trip, but feared it was much more. The incident earlier with U2 and the chanting Hare Krishna's had unleashed something buried in his mind. He began to drift away again, some forgotten thread inside nagging at him. Pulling him on some pathway he'd never recall going down ever before.

An awakening.

Journeys on paths unbidden, a soul's course, and destiny denied like the flashflood down desert canyons, every breath, every step sweeping him away. Thrust to the embrace of fate and futures scrawled into sacred rock. Knowing, the ache of knowing that things were unfolding in the universe all around him and there was nothing he could do. Roger sighed. *This wasn't going to be an ordinary honeymoon was it? I hope whatever happens at least let me get laid tonight first then I'd be open to learning the spiritual pathways of turtles swimming under full moons while fairies caressed their bellies.*

Man, I gotta write this stuff down. Don't know where it is coming from?

He scratched at the hardness forming in his stomach.

They'd made love many times, but he wanted to do it on a Hawaiian beach in the moonlight. Naked, with sand stuck in his cheeks, Blue Hawaiian drinks beside them. Although, intuitively he knew there was little he could do now, except watch it crash into him, into his orderly existence, wiping rationality aside like dust from bookshelves. But the bookshelf didn't exist, and each dust speck was a world unto itself. Nor was the dusting rag just a rag but a curtain of time sweeping all before it, while only chaos talked, reeling in its own hosts. Inevitable things. *Damn, it was like watching the wall approach as your car veers out of control towards it. Again the hymn of angels.*

"We're next, honey."

Hardness in my stomach? What the? Roger tensed, gripping her hand as he rubbed against something in his stomach that shouldn't be there, nor was yesterday.

Yesterday, a Beatles song echoed in the background. *When time was gone away.*

"Ow, you're crushing my hand again. What is wrong?"

"Don't know." *I've done this dozens of times, this is my honeymoon.* He reminded himself he was setting off on his honeymoon with Beth. They were heading for Hawaii and then on a free Grand Canyon whitewater rafting trip he'd won in a company contest last year. He'd promised Bill, his buddy, that he'd also visit Sedona, Arizona. Land of the red rock, canyons and Hopi Indians as part of the package. He shook his head, still not sure why he'd let Bill talk him into going to Sedona, yet something about that name intrigued him, called him. Like this moment, haunted him. What if he said no, *I can't do this. Won't.*

Maybe he should turn around. If he was smart, he would and run before everything he knew up til now in his life melted into a slagheap before his feet.

But destiny was a capricious child at best. Unruly and without definition, no boundaries. No knowing when it would call or where it would surface. Major moments that changed lifetimes and entire nations in the blink of an eye, when a shift of one single belief or thought pattern came without deliberation and totally unexpectedly. Roger held his ground, one foot demanding resolutely to go back and the other? *Into nowhere land.*

"You okay?"

"Yeah, just keep thinking I've forgotten something," he lied. Trying to release her hand, his grip to the now. ***Damn it. Run.***

He stared into her sweet, concerned face. The brown eyes he'd fallen instantly in love with. The petite nose, half-hidden by the cascade of brunette hair, and the twin dimples that erupted with each smile, framing the luscious lips he wanted more than anything to be kissing on a Hawaiian beach.

He shook his head, clearing it, grounding himself with deep breaths, back into his life. His dreams the last few nights had been filled with insights and the dull ache of knowing inevitable things were taking place. Hadn't he read that the big events in one's life are all preordained and in those moments, time slows to a crawl and eternity grips each syllable until half lights shutter away in strobe-lamp fashion? Or was it simply the fact that he was worried about flying, especially after the ISIS and all the constant hysteria induced by the government regarding retaliation or all the conspiracy theories over Covid-19 and government control.

As he stepped through the metal detector he knew.

Everything in his orderly, ordinary, run of the mill, two point five kids, a mortgage, good paying job, benefits, would change.

Fuck, why didn't I run?

Forever.

And ever.

Amen.

Beep. Beep.

Angels snickered and fairies spat magic into the earth before them. Causing new fairies to be born.

Double fuck.

"Sorry, sir. Please go back and remove any coins and other metal objects."

"Oh. Thought I already did that." *The Inevitability of too late to turn back. One path set, the others discarded.* His heart pounded. *Angels were laughing behind my back right now as devilish beings played in the band and others joined in a jig.*

Beth went through while he did as the attendant instructed him, a thorough check of his pockets confirmed that he didn't have any metal on him. The lineup behind him was lengthening, other travelers as eager as he was to set off for their destination waiting patiently. He stepped back through the metal detector's frame again.

Beep. Beep.

The bastards were rolling in the aisles of heaven, howling and whoever held the wild card was gleaming like a jackdaw in heat.

"Over here, sir. Spread your legs and raise your arms. Do you have any metal on your body?" The attendant scanned him with his wand.

"Not that I know of." He wanted to add, *except for the metal plate in my skull,* but he figured anyone who had to stand there doing this job day after day wouldn't have much of a sense of humor. The scene from the movie Spinal Tap came to mind, where the hip rock star with the spray-on leather pants and hefty package bulging from his crotch area is stopped at an airport scanner. Much to the macho dude's chagrin, security discovers a concealed Bierwurst sausage wrapped in tinfoil.

Beep. Beep.

The detector went off around his midsection. "Must be my high-iron diet," he joked weakly, the attendant didn't smile.

"This is no laughing matter sir. Have you had any operations?"

"No, **sir.**" Roger leaned heavily on the "sir". Sweat was breaking out on his forehead. "Never had an operation in my life."

"Proceed to that room over there." *It was now too late to run.*

"Ah, but ... will I miss my flight?"

"Proceed to that room. You have not been cleared for boarding."

"Roger, what's going on here?" Beth stared, frowning, an eye twitching. She hated being singled out in a crowd and he knew he was to blame.

"Don't worry, babe. Something seems to be setting off the metal detectors. I can't board until they check it out." Crap, years later he was still antsy enough after the bombing of the World Trade Towers, and now this. The smirk of chaos commencing its numbing jumbled dance, taking control … the lines between his dream-world and reality blurred. Had he already set something in place that would lead to change? The trouble with inevitable things and chaos is that there's no secretary keeping notes, no Dictaphone to replay the events or a cellphone to take images. Only hands-on experience and he'd never experienced anything deep or religious or wildly spiritual in his life, until now. *Well other than listening to the Orinoco flow by Enya, I knew that listening to that irish bag would get me into trouble. Yet something in her cadence called.*

So where was all this coming from? And why couldn't I shut up that voice in my head?

Three guards lounged in the small room, the two males casually snapped their gum. A rotund female guard sat in the corner reading the **National Enquirer**, scowl pinching her ruddy face. Dealing with her, he sensed, would be like taking sirloin from a pit-bull. It could be done but chances were you'd lose more blood and flesh than you'd gain.

"Hands up. Gotta run another scanner over you," the first male ordered.

It beeped in the same area as before. "Ever have an operation, sir?" The second stared him in the eyes.

"Nope. And I'm a frequent flyer. Never had a problem with security."

"Yeah, got it. Open your shirt, please." The guard was still staring him down. He'd read that police and security personnel were trained to detect if a person was lying just by the way their eyes moved when he was asked a question. Roger stared straight back at the guard as he unbuttoned his shirt.

There, outlined just below his right ribcage, barely visible, was an irregular bulge. The throb he'd scratched at several times, earlier. He turned white; *I should have run, fucking inevitable things. Fucking haloed thy bloody angels.*

"What's that?" The guard poked at him.

Roger winced as he ran his fingers over the area. It wasn't hot to the touch, like he expected a tumor or blood clot to be, nor discolored, in fact it felt smooth, almost metallic. What was it? How'd it get there? Was he going to die? The visions of a woman he'd just seen on TV dying from some sort of viral infection, her body covered in massive sores. The doctors puzzled by this unknown affliction. "I … ah … can only say I've never seen this before." *And that was the bloody truth, how is this possible?*

What the hell was going on here? He'd recently had a physical and his doctor hadn't said anything about this. Surely he would have noticed it himself, in the shower this morning? Wouldn't he?

"So you're standing here trying to tell me you've never seen this before?"

"Yes."

"One more time, sir. Explain to me what that is." The guard raised his voice.

"I … ah … can't. I didn't even know it was there." *Christ, what was this?* Some kind of nightmare? The kind of things that happen only in Sci-Fi movies. The guard held the scanner directly over the lump. It began beeping madly.

"Well, I think you're full of shit myself. I've seen some pretty inventive ways to smuggle things in and out of this country. Ever seen puppies with sown up stomachs, hiding coke? What do you think, Ernie? Dope?" He nodded to the other male.

"Hey, just relax, Burt. We can't assume our mister ready to go on holidays here and relax on a Hawaiian beach sipping Mai Tais is up to something. Maybe he's got some cancerous growth or worse…"

"Oh like the scene from the movie, which one?" He snapped his fingers.

"Alien! Where the baby bursts out from the guys chest."

"Yeah, that's the one." He laughed ignoring the almost shivering Roger, as he kept glancing at the clock on the wall. Ernie turned back to him, all sign of joviality gone. "Nah, you know what I'm thinking? Dope." He eyed him directly again.

The only dopes here were the Dumb and Dumber rejects from security guard school. These were people used to being in control, who enjoyed watching others squirm. This was too surreal, not really happening, like the sensations that had assaulted him as he waited in line, like the hallucinations of marijuana. Like he was floating over all of this and watching, like this was meant to happen, only he didn't know why.

"Dope? How can that be dope, up there?"

"You tell us, sir. But we need to get you checked out. Maybe you've got some kind of explosives taped up inside you, behind some sort of fake skin graft. Never know what these whack job extremist Moslems come up with. Stand behind the screen, remove all your clothing and put on the robe. Over reacting? Remember nine-eleven. I lost an uncle in that pile of rubble and it ain't happening here again on my shift."

"Do I look like a Muslim suicidal type of dude?"

"Don't care, my job is to ensure the national security of this great nation of the US of A. If Trump wants to keep all the Taco breaths out by building a wall, then no wacko is getting in or out past my shift. Prepare the lube Burt and if you give us any more static I'll let Helga over there check you out."

"Or maybe he'd like that," the other laughed.

Roger's ears turned hot. They were baiting him, trying to force him to lose his cool. They were not good people, they liked baiting, torturing others. His intuition was going off, just like at the lineup. He clenched his fists, had to stay calm or goodbye honeymoon, welcome jail cell.

He glanced down at the headlines on the paper Helga was reading, *Man claims aliens impregnated him. Has seven-pound baby girl and two others of unknown DNA.* He finished robing himself in the paper gown and stepped away from the screen. The snap of latex over fingers echoed. The next few minutes weren't going to be quite the honeymoon experience he had planned.

Why in hell didn't I run, when my guts told me to?

Chapter Two

*I*n *the hallway, four humans, intent on killing me.* Her internal honed senses pulsed danger. Sherida opened her eyes and leap from her bed. She didn't have to glance at the clock to know it was 3:12 a.m. Her internal senses already knew that.

Naked; no time to dress. Sherida dove across the pitch-black hotel room, grabbing her laser from its holster as a moment later the hotel room door burst open. She slid up against the dresser. The flash of light from the hallway behind them highlighted the intruders as they tried to shoulder their way in. Hushed bursts from handguns equipped with silencers thumped her bed; still warm from her body.

Someone reached for the light switch. With her mind she closed the door to the suite, trapping two of the men outside in the corridor. In the same instant she shot out the light. Her infra-red vision kicked in automatically, a precious advantage. Two more bursts from her laser pierced the door, forming twin smoking pinholes where she sensed the heat of the two men. Her mind's senses registered their heats stopping and their life essences leave their bodies.

"Where?" He spun around and fired a bullet randomly into the darkness. Sherida didn't utter a sound as the bullet grazed her shoulder.

"Shit! I can't see shit! Behind..." were the last words of the other two inside the dark hotel room as two more bursts of white intensity seared all life from them. They thumped to the floor.

Sherida stood, her senses scanning the area assuring her that there were no others on this floor, but they had backup. She tore a strip from the bed and wrapped her shoulder to stem the blood as her internal repair devices began to kick in. Six others were waiting outside, about to enter the hotel. Clean-up crew, waiting for a signal or no signal depending on what happened in her room. Time was of the essence. She moved around as if her surroundings were illuminated by daylight and not cast in blackness, thankful that she couldn't see with her eyes the blood splattering the carpet and the bodies as she frisked them. No ID, no way of discovering where they came from or who had sent them. Someone wanted her dead. More importantly, someone knew she was on Earth. Sending this number of men after her wasn't about some kind of local gangster clash mix-up. This was someone like herself, not from this world.

This changed completely everything. If someone knew about her, maybe they knew about the others. She'd have to check and make sure her contacts were okay. Her circuits had already kicked in to seal the flesh wound. She closed her eyes and a dark casual pantsuit covered her. Noises were starting up in the hallway, she sensed the apartment to her left was empty and even though this took an enormous drain on her systems she willed herself thorough the wall and left via the next suite as the humans began to mill about staring at the two dead biker types littering the hallway. Someone screamed.

Outside in the alleyway a deep breath of grounding energy washed over her and she closed her eyes. Using her omniscient vision she pictured herself staring down at herself and then pictured everything around her within the next couple of blocks. The buzz of human energy presented nothing of a problem. For now she was safe, other than the others after her, were entering the hotel. She tried to contact home-base but couldn't, the link wasn't working.

Odd?

That had never happened since she'd joined the angels so many years ago. That was a secured, dimensional line, supposedly unbreakable. Which meant that also home-world didn't know where she was or if she was okay.

She was cut off for now. Someone or something had interfered with her, her mission and it had nearly cost her life. She'd find out who it was. As for the other eleven? No way of contacting them either.

Closing her eyes Sherida allowed her body to shimmer, shutting down all functions except biological repair and remote monitoring. She had to deplete the huge drain on her energies as she shifted into out of time sequence, becoming invisible. *Repair myself first and then begin looking for answers.*

Several hours later a being dressed in black long distinguished raincoat shimmered into view on Union Street in Seattle. His face hidden behind the upturned hood shimmered from slotted red cornea eyes and long reptilian nose into a Caucasian male. Zolnar stared around him catching the sensations of the street scene. His first time on Earth.

It appears the first wave had failed to eliminate all the angels, including the female one called Sherida. She was good, elusive, but not for long. He pressed a button and his image shimmered again and transformed into a middle-aged white male wearing an Armani suit that just walked by him. *Now the inbred thrill of the hunt began, he* wrinkled his nose. *Disgusting how they still burned fossil fuels on this world.* He coughed. *No wonder they lived such a short time.*

He stepped onto the sidewalk and bumped against a passerby, his stomach turning. *Zagnet and double Zagnet, such a revolting smell these flesh eaters gave off.* His kind hadn't done that for centuries, perfecting synthesizing proteins over thousands of years ago, although the prospect of eating meat and raw flesh again seemed suddenly appealing. Carnivore's traits, an ancient reptilian desire, the hunt. He knew some of his kind still went on illegal hunts. He dialed in a number and felt the wash of chemicals into his system, settling his stomach instantly. Enough of that, once he achieved his goals, he could do whatever he desired, a little hunting trip now seemed like a very delicious thought.

Zolnar checked his scanner. Indeed, some angels had proven very resourceful, they were well trained and difficult to kill. Although he knew the landing locations for all of them, a couple seemed not to rely on links to the home world. Each he knew were trained totally different depending on the continent and person they had to observe.

Odd, but it would only a matter of time before he tracked those down. A beep came in. *Good.* The one he was worried about the most in the area called Europe had been eliminated. *Good everything is proceeding just marvellously.*

Jet engines roared overhead as Roger sat down gingerly in the cab. The flight he and Beth were supposed to be on was taxiing down the run. *What a lousy start to a honeymoon.* The petroleum jelly gurgled again in his bowels.

"You okay?" His new wife sent him a sympathetic smile.

He stared into her sweet, concerned face as he frowned and gripped her hand. "I think so, but if our cabbie hangs too fast a right, he might have a rather unpleasant experience in the back of his cab. You're probably wondering what the hell is going on, and just how well do I know this guy?"

Her brown eyes he'd fallen instantly in love with smiled back. Her nervous smile didn't hide the dimples that erupted, framing luscious lips he wanted more than anything to be kissing on a sunset beach instead of clamping his butt cheeks together over every bump that threatened to expel even more of the gurgling mass brewing inside him. He'd already gone twice rather explosively in the bathroom.

"It crossed my mind, but first we need to get you to the doctor. Let's look at the bright side, handsome. We got lucky. You weren't arrested as a terrorist."

"Ah, thanks sweetheart, I think that dawned on those dimwits after I said I was leaving the country, not entering it. Only the problem is, I'm not sure what this is all about, or what this is inside me and until I get some answers to this, this ... disaster," he shook his head, "I might not be allowed back on an airplane. I can't believe you're taking this so cool on our honeymoon." Roger squinted as pain shot up his insides over another dip in the road.

Beth smiled, her dimples showing. "Hey! You forget I married you because I love you, for better or worse, lubricated or non-lubricated bowels." She giggled. "I think it'll make a great story for our kids. So what's the verdict? Are you going to be okay?" They hadn't had time to talk much until now.

"If I survive this taxi ride, after the rectal probing and two pounds of jelly."

"Can't say I've ever had the pleasure of a jelly enema."

"Well, it wasn't on my list of ten things in my bucket list that I want to experience in this lifetime. Nor to do on my honeymoon either. It's funny, I can't feel anything and I wouldn't even know I've got a hunk of metal in me, except when I touch it. On their x-rays the mass is solid, probably not non-organic as nothing shows through it, they suspected metal, lead perhaps. Whatever this mass is it's solid."

"So what is …?"

"Ah, geez!" The jelly kept oozing down, no matter how hard a death-grip his rear end made on the seat.

"Leaking, are we?" Beth snickered.

"Not funny, Beth. They must have used half a tube of jelly on me. Don't think I'm going to make it." Roger shuffled as delicately as he could, clamping his butt cheeks together. "I'm sure as hell not going through this again. Not exactly the type of holiday penetration I expected. Cabbie, pull into that 7-11 quick."

"Nice tush, hon." Beth gave him a small pat on the rear as he yanked open the door, walking as fast as he calmly could for the restrooms. Audible gurgles could be heard in the cab coming from Roger's stomach.

Beth smiled as the cab driver stared up. "It's our honeymoon, he's very shy and nervous, a virgin actually."

The dark-skinned cabbie stared in disbelief, "Wow, at his age, must have led a sheltered life."

"Yeah, one of them Mormon type colonies I stole him away from." She lied hoping he wouldn't be long as the meter ticked away. They still had an hour to make it to the on-call doctor and three before the rescheduled flight. Which hadn't cost a fortune as the airline had people on reserve to jump into their place. How he didn't know there was a hunk of metal, however small stuck in him though is perplexing.

Tom yawned as he struggled into his office. *Eleven a.m.! Far too early for a Monday morning.* He buzzed his secretary for coffee and sank into the confines of his padded leather chair. "Oh."

He hid his head in his hands. *Too much coke or too much booze. Or Both.*

It had been a good night. Maybe he should call his apartment and see if that hot brunette was still there. He punched the numbers on his phone but hung up. "Damn, was it Denise or Diane? Could go for round two with that one." He smiled to himself as Melinda, his secretary, walked in.

"How's the man-whore doing this afternoon?" she joked.

Melinda knew him too well; they'd been working together for nearly two years. He had tried to put the moves on her many times, until he discovered she was more into women. "Anytime you want to switch to one hundred percent real beef, let me know."

"If I ever do, it won't be with you. I choke on small bones. Wouldn't want to get anything stuck between my teeth."

"Still a crying shame. Nice toilet," he muttered as she walked out of the room studying her rear. She always wore the tightest skirts. Except for the rings in her eyebrow and lip, he found her very appealing, but at least her sexual preference kept their relationship on a strictly business level. He'd picked up more chicks since she started working here. She was also not only good at her job but especially useful for finding out what women liked, particularly in bed. After all, who better to ask than a dyke?

Sipping on his coffee he stared at his office walls: posters, photographs, sets of Tycomonster cards and other memorabilia, all successful marketing products he'd designed. A salesman, good at knowing what the public craved or thought they did, or making them desire certain products, all essential selling skills in this field.

High on the day's agenda was the biggest project he was working on, marketing schemes for the new Galaxy Warriors movie series due next spring. His company had been awarded the contract with six figures being his share, plus a percentage. Should sit well in his bank account and keep him in coke and beautiful women for a while.

With another yawn he sorted through the mail Melinda had plopped on his desk. Mostly junk from wannabes proposing already-done crap. The first package contained a set of animal pictures. "Too cute." He attached a standard response letter and set the package in Melinda's outgoing mail slot to have the tastefully attached, thanks but not quite right for us standard letter so many proposals got. The next envelope contained photos of couples engaged in orgies. "Too racy." He attached the same response letter but figured he'd keep the pictures for further perusal on nights when he alone. Which wasn't many lately.

On went the morning until Melinda buzzed him. "Don't forget you've got lunch at twelve at Manhattan's."

"Did I ever tell you for a lezbo chick you're alright?"

"Did I ever tell you for a male pig, you're absolutely disgusting?"

He cut off the mike before she could finish her 'fuck you' response. Tom grabbed his briefcase and the rest of the mail, which he could open before his client arrived, if he left now. He hadn't eaten this morning, so lunch and a few coffees would go down well, not to mention a stiff shot of rye.

At the restaurant, sipping on his usual liquid lunch, he ripped open the last of his mail. He got a lot of samples and products issues from companies and people hoping he could make them rich. Most were a waste of his time, or already done. A heavy package containing several six-by-eight cards tore apart too easily. Some slipped out and fell to the floor.

"Damn," he muttered, bending over to pick them up and waving to snag the waitress's attention. He turned the card over and stared into the scene it represented. A hologram, unlike anything he'd ever seen. Crystal blue waves crashing on the beach before him. Cries of seagulls overhead. His toes curled into the grittiness of the hot sand. Hibiscus and Lei scents filled the air. Heat, blistering heat. He shielded his eyes. The stench of salt air and rotting seaweed assailed his nostrils. He wiped at sweat beading on his forehead, blinked and was pulled back into the restaurant.

"Jesus Christ," he muttered and stared into the card again. The same vision filled his world, engulfing every sense in his body. He was again on this beach! Seagulls cried out overhead.

"Excuse me, I haven't got all day. We're one short and I'm covering eight other tables. Hello!" the waitress barked, clad in a bikini and dinner tray.

Tom shook his head and set the card down. "In-frigging-credible. Tell me, what do you see in this picture?"

"Look, I don't have time to screw around with a postcard of a beach..." The empty tray fell from her fingers fell from her hand as she staggered back.

"It pulled me in. Holy shit. I was there." She blinked in disbelief as she started to pick up the tray she'd dropped.

"Hey, can a guy get a damn coffee in this place or what?" Someone from another table yelled.

"I'll be right there." She retrieved her tray, ignoring the yammering patron. "What was that?"

"Just a new laser Three-D hologram I'm working on," he lied, making up the first thing that came into his head. "What do you think?"

"Amazing. I was on that beach. That's a sure-fire winner, mister."

"Yeah, what I thought." Tom searched the package for a letter. All it said was that he had ten days to view the product before responding, after which it would be offered to another agency. It was from a company he'd never heard of, Unearthly Creations, which in his line of work wasn't too unusual: a lot of fly-by-the-seat-of-your-pants companies were out there. At the bottom was an email address: UnearthlyCreations@universe.com.

"This is good, frigging good." Tom slapped fifty bucks on the table and yelled at the waitress, "There'll be two gentlemen arriving to meet me in about ten minutes. Tell them I had a family emergency and I'll get my secretary to reschedule for later this week. I left money on the table and a good tip. Thanks."

He threw the photos into his briefcase and ran for the door, buzzing Melinda on his cell phone. "Melinda, cancel or reschedule any appointments I have this afternoon."

"But you're booked solid."

"Cancel them. I need to deal with something incredible that just got dumped in my lap. I'll be at home on my computer."

"This better be good, for all the shit I'm going to have to go through."

"Honey, this is hot stuff, real hot."

Chapter Three

*A*t certain times in our lives a rare wind blows across the fields of our minds that like others before it, stirs leaves and rustles grasses. Only this breeze disturbs dust covering dormant memories thought buried beneath the weight of time's passage. Stricken chords begin vibrations, opening barbs of echoes nagging at the consciousness. Singing to voices thought gone from previous incarnations, former lives and sequestered dreams.

As dust settles and the wind diminishes, illusions present themselves that everything appears the same as before. Except the eyes and their four accompanying cohorts are in a sense easily deceived fools, allowing self-absorbed egos to bask in their own vanities. Oblivious to the fact that evolution is an aching compulsion beckoning with greater urgency at every passing breath to let change occur naturally. While within, the subconscious relentlessly hammers away at logic's walls with persistent scratches of intuition's voice.

Calling out to the settling dust, that as the wind quiets, something has inexplicably changed.

And as the stirred leaf is returned to its former position, awakenings take root in the realization, beneath knowing's furtive glances, that it can never be put back into the same state of cognizance as before.

Expelling the old self and inhaling the new is all part of the process, the rhythmicity of life, like the waves of the ocean stealing at the shore's foundation of imposed truths.

In the Akashic Hall of Records I look up from the Tome, my mind inscribing astral light thoughts onto the blank pages set before me. "Why am I here?" I ask.

The Hathor guide moves behind me. "Sundering one's self from the whole and from All That Is brings not truly understanding, not knowing Thyself." He glances at my words. "You begin to understand this final Chakra lesson well. It is time for this teacher to leave, for there is no more I can show you."

I have learned much from him, with so much left to learn. He vanishes as I finish writing. In the scheme of universal matters, even time itself, becomes meaningless.

My mind begins to recite some more in this my final lesson before?

Unknown.

Yet enlightenment cannot be won without darkness and from that void comes the sacred knowledge that there is no going back, no retreating from awareness, for that surely leads on the path to madness. We have both inside, light and dark, awareness and ignorance. To deny one means to surrender to the other and that is one of the secrets in transcending this realm and in comprehending the existence of the others.

*Still, somewhere on awareness' wind comes the tongues of chaos humming an endless incantation, as surely as old people whisper and children laugh freely, that nothing, **absolutely nothing**, is as we remembered it.*

Nor can it ever be as it once was as the winds of chaos swirl.

"That wind blew this morning as you chose to open this book," his voice echoes from above reseeding into the darkness.

Thanks for nothing, bloody transcendental dimensional level 6.3 teachers. Roger slammed the light emitting dimensional volume closed or as closed as voluminous light can be. Sparkles erupted upwards in tingling vibrations.

Why the fuck couldn't I have stuck to selling insurance. No instead I'm trying to guarantee the insurance of our continued existence as a species of evolved monkey beings happy with shagging our brains out, playing virtual computer games and eating fast food?

Did Buddha ever have days like these?

"'Come to Sedona,'" Bill told me. 'You'll be amazed by the energy of this place.'" Roger squinted from beneath the shade of his newspaper, sweat pouring down his brow. "I'm amazed by the buckets of sweat I'm producing, that's what I'm amazed by." *How does anyone in their right or even in their left minds choose to live here or stay here?*

Beth stood by, "Quit complaining, these guys are dancing in full regalia and they're not sweating half as much as you."

"They're used to it. I bet they move up to Seattle and experience the occasional five below zero and they'd be dressed in four pairs of long johns and three parkas." He laughed pulling another bead of sweat from his eyebrows.

In the background groups of Hopi gathered around large leather topped drums chanting and wailing in time to their pounding away with leather wrapped sticks. Dancers had begun to enter the plaza dressed in bright colored Aztec style of costumes, some bearing head dresses looking like spaceman helmets adorned with eagle feathers and ferns. Grass skirts swished as rattles shook the air. Others bore long curvy horns of antelope, decked in the white of eagle down. "Oraibi two horned priests, very sacred," someone nudged him in the crowd of gawkers.

Roger knew one thing as he shielded his eyes. That dream last night was of his calling to this place. But it wasn't about darkness and cooling. "Crap, Bill's right about the energy thing out here.

The sun's energy, that is. Right now I sure wish I'd brought some sunblock, 600 strength." Bill had insisted that if he was coming to the Grand Canyon he had to visit Sedona and the Hopi Reservation. He had told him about his visit here as a teenager, the red rock and the spiritual energy. Right now the only thing Roger would find deeply spiritual would be a glass of ice-cold Millers beer. *That's my kind of religion.*

"Bill? The guy who talks about weird stuff like karma, alien abduction and chakras? He talked you into coming here?" Beth blinked from under her straw hat.

"No, that would be Theodore. Bill just likes to smoke dope and pretend he sees auras when he's stoned. Worked well when we were teens trying to pick up chicks," Roger laughed. "I don't know why but it twigged something inside and my guts told me I had to come. Come on, at least we get to see some neat dancers. I'll show you a good time tonight when I slather you all over naked with Aloe Vera to calm the sunburn."

"Well, you've sure got some strange friends. All I see here is red rock, red dust, red canyons, red shimmering heat and not one ice cold beer in sight. Or in my case one glass of deep red wine, room temp or chilled. I'm not fussy. " Beth fanned herself. "At least when we were white-water rafting on the Canyon yesterday the water was a cooler and refreshing. Speaking of refreshing, the only thing red I really desire right now would be a glass of Merlot and if I get anymore sunburnt you ain't coming anywhere near me." She fanned herself.

"Yeah, whitewater rafting in the heat of the summer when ice cold water hits you in hundred degree heat and you can feel your balls shrivel up your throat. Hey, come on, after this we're going home. Let's enjoy the last couple of days of our honeymoon. This and the airport thing may be a fiasco, but the rest had been a riot." He winked at her. Beth smiled shyly back.

Thanks to the fiasco at the airport, they were lucky to have had a honeymoon at all. After he'd been denied boarding Beth had whisked him off to his doctor, who had taken X-rays that showed nothing until the wattage on the machine was increased, revealing a piece of metal. Almost like it had been sitting there the whole time, waiting to be discovered. Roger had demanded that he cut it out. The doctors insisted it would be any easy operation, no complications, and that he could fly the next day. They were $1200 poorer between the rebooking of the flights and the medical fees, but he wasn't prepared to deny Beth their honeymoon.

So now the two-inch piece of metal was sitting in a jar on his mantel, posing the nagging question: how does one carry such a thing on his body and not feel it? More importantly, how'd it get there? He'd mention it to Theodore when he got back, that man knew practically everything about woo-woo stuff and spiritual matters. And even more about non-Gaia born creatures. *If anyone was to tell me he's an alien in disguise I wouldn't be at all surprised.*

Although for one he was glad that it was something metallic and not a tumor or worse. He rubbed gently at the irritation of the dissolving sutures. At least the operation hadn't interfered with any of his performances on their honeymoon nights, now that would have sucked.

Roger watched the performers sweeping through the plaza, twirling and strutting to ancient rhythms and tribal songs regarding the upcoming harvest season. He was surprised that under that heavy gear they could even move, let alone dance. Why had he come here, other than because he'd won that free rafting trip? Being nailed by forty something degree water in a 124-degree day was thrilling, but nothing he'd want to do on a regular basis. Beth had loved it. Trying to sleep on a double cot inches above the scalding sand hadn't been very restful either, especially when scorpions were known to lurk beneath the rocks and scuttle into warm cavities. *Another creature that god invented on a night out drinking with the guys to piss everyone else off.*

He yawned, at least they had a real bed to sleep in tonight with chilled beer and wine in the fridge. Beth wasn't one for the great outdoors normally, her idea of roughing it was a motel without room service.

One of the Kachina dancers of the Hopi people caught his eye. Unlike the others who wore hats shaped like stick people, this figure's squared head was covered with stark black and white Eagle feathers, some sprouting from behind. Streaks of ochre and black paint, and what looked like blood, completed a facemask that bore two huge round black eyes and a round black mouth full of white fangs, surrounded by scarlet shards of glass. Hanging from a long cloak of furs, skinned rabbits dangled, bouncing in a pantomime of dance, and on its belt hung a gourd. In one hand the dancer held a stick Roger recognized as a native planting stick, and in the other a stylized replica of a blazing torch.

"Why would the Hopi put such an ugly thing in their festival? I thought these ceremonial dances were meant to attract tourists, not scare them off," Beth commented.

As if hearing her, the figure approached. The pad of its feet rippled through Roger's senses. He blinked, the suddenness of last nights dream tore into his vision. It stopped and danced before them, its black eyes staring directly at Roger. *Padding, was it him in my dreams?*

Roger blinked, trying to stagger back out from the calling of the visions that were swirling in his mind trying to issue forth.

"Honey, I think it wants us to take its picture." Beth whipped out her camera and snapped off a half-dozen shots, they'd have a lot of pictures to download when they got home. Good thing he'd bought a spare couple of cards.

She collared the couple next to them to take a picture of them beside the dancer, who merely wavered in front of him. The mists of dreamtime playing a supple tone on his consciousness calling to him, like a lion calling to the blood of the gazelle.

Roger shook his head pulling himself back into the cruel heat of the day. Whatever this was about, he didn't know. But that bizarre being, he tried to see behind the cutouts of the mask, but it was designed to conceal the performer's eyes. Because he was almost certain whatever it was, human and Gaia born didn't fit its DNA.

Finally the dance ended and the figure shook the fire-stick at him, the great black eyes boring into him as it breathed heavily, gasping like a fish out of water.

"Honey, this is kinda freaky." Beth clutched at his arm.

"Ah, nice costume, great performance. Thanks for the picture," Roger smiled and began to push her and him away as echoes within called for release.

"Bahanna." It finally spoke in a deep baritone voice that made both of them jump. "You who have traveled many lands in the last days, know this."

How the heck did it know that? Probably just a good guess, being both were beat red, slathered in lotion and not a natural dusky brown of the natives.

"Most of you Bahannas trample the Earth, use it like tissue paper and throw it aside. But among your kind on this third-dimensional plane are those who play out their lives living meekly in harmony with the Earth and all of creation. Many others become addicted to material pleasure, be it pursuit of money or the baser gratification of drugs or alcohol. The rarer ones desire more and seek answers. Some use that knowledge as wisdom to enhance their lives and the lives of those around them, and others freely bridge worlds, dimensions and realms. Calling themselves here. Those ones are extremely rare, like our shamans. Gateway walkers to answer the calling."

"Huh? Honey if this part of their ceremonies, it's a small wonder they get anyone out here. Let's go, he's scaring me."

"Agreed." That went way over his head. "Some kind of Hopi mumbo jumbo they probably spewed to all of the tourists." Although the term 'gateway walker' stuck, boring into his mind like a laser. Calling to a place inside that remembered.

"You're not ready yet. If you're meant too, at some point you'll understand and the teachings will begin." It answered his not asked question, beckoning from deep inside.

"Understand, I haven't a damn clue what the hell he's talking about. I don't know of any teachings… "

"Techqua Ikachi!" An explosion of firecrackers, staccato crackles, drew Roger and Beth's attention away. When he turned back the dancer was gone. He scanned the crowd, spotted him weaving through a mass of people beating a hasty retreat from this ceremony and this realm, he sensed without realizing what he just thought to himself.

"Honey, what was that all about?" Beth sidled up against him as the fireworks ended.

"Who knows?" Voices inside, began their chanting, talking of chaos and futures unwritten. Stirring the depths of murky water, raising things from his dreams of the other night. "A chance meeting between strangers, a prelude to futures unexplored," he murmured. "To be, ode to be. Of things unseen."

Beth gaped at him. "What? I really hate it when you begin spouting woo-woo things and Shakespearian quotes from your college days. Although I bet it used to get a few chicks with pickup lines like that. Man, I really got to get inside your head. I bet Buddha dreams to you on a regular basis smoking one fat doobie."

"Well that was pretty profound on your part. I think it was poetry I read somewhere, Shakespeare, or Tennyson I think," he lied, yet the words he knew had come from within. From some memory, buried until now in his soul. Roger shook his head trying to stay present. He felt like he was being pulled away from here, just as he had been while waiting in line at the airport. Something trying to find him. *Those moments of unknown things approaching. God I hate it when I get these and I've been getting them a lot since coming here or at least since the metal was found in me. The metal I wonder?*

"Really, you scare me sometimes."

"I'm beginning to scare myself." Destinies; seeking him like chaos drumming in the sudden crack of violent thunder and hail searing all beneath its touch.

I can't keep these thoughts out of my head. I need a stiff drink to quiet it up.

The figure was now on the other side of the plaza. This had been one strange holiday. Talk about expect the unexpected, truth being stranger than fiction and all that.

As they left the plaza Roger excused himself to use the washroom. As he was relieving himself, an old native man walked in and used the next urinal. They were as far as he knew the only two.

"Enjoying the Niman ceremonies?" he asked.

"The what?"

"The Going Home ceremonies."

"I was," he paused, *thinking I shouldn't really be talking to a stranger of deep spiritual matters while holding my dick in my hand. But then so was he.* "Until I had a strange experience. One of the dancers, was dressed in such a grotesque costume. I thought you wanted to attract tourists, not freak them out."

The old man grunted as he released his stream. "That one represents Maasaw. He came to us around 1100 AD."

"Why does he look so bizarre and ferocious?" *and remotely unhuman. Not usually the place to be a center of learning, I'd expect that in a library or our mosque not in front of a smelly urinal. But there is that old saying, the teacher attracts the pupil.*

"It is the Creator's way. He is not of this world. One must see past illusion to the truth. Everything is illusion. You must trust your inner sense, not your eyes. Not everything that looks terrifying is, and not everything that looks harmless is as well. Most of us see through the eyes and the eyes are the greatest deceivers. The Creator told us to trust our inner selves, our intuitive abilities. Our people did, and then he taught us many wonderful things, including how to harvest corn."

How could you see without your eyes?

"Maasaw also gave us prophesies. You should read about them. All have come true, which means the predicted end of this, the fourth cycle, is close at hand."

"The who? Prophesies? Like what?" *Hopi craziness, is this what Bill meant? And it obviously hadn't ended yet.* Roger shook himself and strolled to the sinks as the cascade of rank urine still cracked the washrooms air.

Man that old guy has one huge bladder.

"He predicted the two world wars, and a third one. He predicted the coming of the Bahanna, white man to our lands, a being disconnected from the cycles of Mother Earth, who speaks with forked tongue and will not rest until the last native is gone. He said there would be horseless carriages and moving houses of iron. That men would be able to speak through space and through cobwebs. That there will be roads in the sky. That women would be devalued, that their skirts would rise above the knees and they would take over men's clothing. That one day our own children will become our enemies. That the mother villages will be destroyed and all of Earth will become unbalanced by the actions of the Bahanna. All of these actions will cause the ending of the fourth cycle, and when the white man who took our corner of the powerstone returns it to complete the tablet of the Fire Clans, the fifth cycle will start. That will be the last sign before the closing of this cycle. According to Maasaw the world we know travels around the outside of our galaxy and completes that journey every 25,920 years, to line up again with the eye of God."

Hadn't ended? This nutcase seemed to just be getting started and he was still peeing away. They must hold their waters within for days. "Whew, that's quite a hatful of predictions. When did you say this Maasaw came here?"

"Around 1100 AD." The old man stopped. Shook himself once and walked out without washing his hands or even saying anything profound or stupid, *like have a nice life.*

Let me guess, cleanliness is but an illusion of dirtiness. Roger stood there at the sink, pondering. *So what then am I supposed to be seeing beyond my vision?*

All that we see or seem, is but a dream, within a dream.
Edgar Allen Poe

A quote from my university days: maybe I was just beginning to understand what Poe was saying. If this was all a dream, where and what was reality? That's what I needed to ask the old man, that and gateways. That crackpot dancer had mentioned something about being a Gateway Walker. That's what I wanted to ask him. Roger hurried out of the washroom and nearly ran over Beth standing just outside.

"Sorry, I just wanted to talk to that old guy who just left."

"What old guy? You've been in there forever. No one has come out of that washroom. I was ready to barge in, thinking you'd passed out from the heat and I'd find you face down in a urinal."

"The old native guy. Red bandana around his head, dirty long gray hair, long smock covering most of him. He was just in there, walked out a minute ago without washing his hands."

"Read my lips, you are losing it. NO ONE, came in or out since you did. I've been standing here wilting, waiting for you since you went in. Sure you haven't inhaled any of that peyote these natives smoke?"

"No one. So you're saying I was in there alone?"

She smiled back. "Well unless he did a native version of Mary Poppins and vanished up the chimney and I don't see any stacks around here."

He blinked in utter disbelief. *This day just got even more fucked up.* "Crap, maybe the heat's getting to me. I thought I was talking to this old native guy. The heat must be getting to me. I think I was just talking to an apparition."

"Or the penis in your hand, men."

The old man's words echoed: *illusions, this world is of illusions, don't trust your eyes, trust what the voice inside is telling you.*

"I guess Edgar has a point," he muttered to himself. "Say, let's get out of the sun and grab some chow before heading over to Boynton Canyon."

"You still want to do that meditating thing? I'm feeling pretty tired from this heat. After lunch I just want to lie down for a while." Beth rubbed a well-used cloth over her forehead.

Bill had told him that the most powerful and mystical place around here was the Canyon. Roger hadn't intended to, thought it was all too spooky, but now …. Besides, something was nagging at him, something the first native, the dancer, had said. He'd mentioned gateway walkers. What had he meant by that? *Apparently, whatever he meant I wasn't ready for it. Whatever IT was? Yeah, Bill hadn't let me down, this land was pretty bizarre with some unique energy that keeps calling to me.* He remembered the old native man shaking his willy, a smile on his face like he knew he triggered something deep within me before he disappeared. *If he was actually here to begin with and I hadn't made him up? Only, what truly just happened this afternoon? No, he was there. I didn't imagine him up from nowhere.* He shook his head. *Buddha, how you made it through this crazy woo woo'd shit is beyond me.*

Another one of those weird moments trembling in timelines I don't know where it's going. Yup, sure some honeymoon this is turning out to be. Expect the unexpected, would make for the great title of some sci-fi series which is starting to turn out to be my life. Crap, I guess selling insurance is not my real reason for being here. Only why was I really here.

Gateway Walker.

Two words calling at him.

Chapter Four

"*W*elcome. Tiyah said you'd be coming. Are you ready?"

"*Ready?*" *I turn and looked into the face of a tall being towering over me, its hair pulled back to reveal elongated pointy ears. Where the hell was I? Is this a dream, am I in some kind of bizarre dream time?*

The being wore flowing luminous robes and held a large book in hands of grace and delicateness. Its smile radiated love and kindness. I felt them washing over me.

"Follow me, if you're ready to begin the teachings."

"Ready? For what? Teachings? I don't understand." Yet inside I did. I knew what this being was asking of me, what Tiyah had asked and the truly weird part, I haven't met her yet. A new stage of life, of growing, had begun. As I walked calmly behind the tall lithesome being I knew I was changing my life, going down a path that would make everything I had learned so far meaningless, yet give me more meaning than I'd ever known.

It came to me, He was a Hathor, they were beyond names, so I just called him Hathor. Teachers of a higher order that were engaged by others to guide them on spiritual journeys. How did I intuitively know that and where were we?

The Hathor guided me through the grounds of the complex. At one point I turned and stared at the imposing structure of a step pyramid a mile or so off in the distance. Jungle surrounded the area, although it had been cleared from the courtyard we walked in. So much like the Temple of the Sun complex at Teotihuacan. In one stride we were halfway across the courtyard, in another at the base of the pyramid, and as I put my foot down to climb the first rise we were on top of the three hundred and sixty five steps and overlooking the entire jungle. For all I knew we could have been there sometime in bygone centuries. "How?"

"Time is the constant of the third dimension. Not so with other realms." It spoke inside my mind.

"But it is so bewildering, confusing."

"Only those not used to it see chaos here. Everything is the way it is meant to be. Order is a matter of perception. Chaos is a way of focusing."

I shook my head. "This is so hard to wrap my brain around. Things happening so fast." I blinked, gripping the edge of a stone railing, staring down from the dizzying heights of this pyramid. "Is that why you are here? Are you to teach me something about the other dimensions?"

"I am a teacher and your spirit guide from the realms beyond this one. But don't get me wrong, it is not I that called you. It is you that called me."

"Say what? I didn't call you." I thought I was just getting some sleep after a bewildering day.

"Think again. Did you not summon the one your kind calls a shaman of the wood stick with the fish of many teeth?"

"Charlie? But I met him only after watching an article on TV." I stopped, realizing I was talking about someone else I hadn't met yet either. How was this possible? "He was just there by …"

"Coincidence?"

It had picked the exact word out of my head. "Hey. Are you reading my thoughts?"

"No. It's just that your thoughts spill out faster than a torrent. It is like a waterfall, you are shouting so loudly in my mind."

"Before I say it, I'll bet you were about to say."

"*Exactly. Originally you called Sherida, but you also called the shaman, you called Tiyah, and you called me.*"

Tiyah, the name struck a chord. "*Tiyah, the Egyptian lady at the pyramid and Stonehenge? How do I call people, I don't know, haven't met yet? That is not possible?*" *But he did know her, the shaman and Sherida, his guardian angel. This shouldn't be possible.*

"*It is and she knows these power centers well, since she helped build them. Tiyah was originally a keeper of the crystals.*"

"*Say what? Helped build? But she's young, couldn't be much over --*"

"*Sixty thousand years young, of your Earth time, nearly half her lifespan. She is a teacher of your places of learning called the Mystery Schools.*"

"*She mentioned the Mystery Schools. Are they related, then, to the pyramids?*"

"*There is much that you will find out, and much that I cannot tell you, yet. It would wreck the learning and the journey.*"

"*I'm beginning to see that patience is a good thing to have out here.*" *I would think that being sixty thousand years old one would develop a lot of patience.*

"*You are learning fast. But I've said enough. We are not here to speak of other matters today. My purpose is to teach you of the fourth dimension and the beginning is to understand the centers within you.*"

"*Centers?*"

"*Power centers. The energy that spins inside that keeps you in touch with the rest of the universe. You must become knowledgeable of your internal chakras, as they are called here, before you can walk in the gateways to other worlds.*"

"*How did you know about the gateway thing? Let me guess, I called you, so you are a teacher of gateway walkers.*"

"*Ah, you are perceptive after all.*"

He may have thought I was perceptive, but I didn't have the foggiest idea what was remotely going on here. All I knew about Chakras is that Buddhists sat around painting their faces and chanting a lot, probably strung out on some hallucinogenic herbs like marijuana.

Yet there was much that made sense, in mixed up weird sort of way.

He started to walk and before I knew it we'd walked down into the heart of the pyramid from a flight of stairs located in the small room on top. Protrusions of shell-like objects glowed as we walked, the energy of our bodies, I assumed, causing them to turn on so like the crystals in that cave I entered recently in Boynton canyon. Yet, this place was vaguely ...

"I've ... I've been here before," I blurted. The Hathor said nothing as I stared harder at the walls. Some of the blocks were inscribed, or chiseled. I peered closer. "This corridor, these carvings on the walls, this is a classroom."

"Yes it is. And in other lifetimes, you have been here."

"Other lifetimes? But that's impossible, I've never been here before. I've never seen ..."

I stopped, peering at a certain inscription. The brief vision of myself, chiseling away in a feverish pitch, trying to finish the plaque before ...

"Before what?" The stone figures gazed out with large eyes, so much like the beings on the totem. "Why was that so important?"

"Something to ponder over another time. But you chose to stand next to the tablet of the Muladhara Chakra. The first chakra, indeed most auspicious of you for this is where we begin the journey."

I stared up at the tablet above the one that had triggered the flashback and ran my fingers over the carved edges. "I know these." Four lotus petals touching each other and within a square. Each petal had symbols, sacred symbols, inscribed within. Soft vibrations began in the background as I ran my fingers over them, returning to the first and beginning again. Words, some sort of chant, wanted to echo from my lips.

"The touching and repeating of these are designed to begin the necessary vibrations to open the root chakra."

"I know this." Sounds, like the calls of whales, echoed in the background. A xylophone-like instrument chimed, playing one long note after another.

I turned and the being known as the Hathor was gone, its voice drifting away like mist on water. Alone, I returned to run my fingers over the stone.

"You carved those also." From the darkness came one final echo. "More than any, this chakra is of the earth."

"Of grounding and survival," I muttered. The root that anchored all others. Without this one as a solid foundation, like the basement to a mansion, nothing could withstand, nor stay together. The fragrance of cedar filled the air as I ran my fingers over this tablet, which began to glow a dull red. All the other chakras flowed through this one. Without even knowing where the image sprang from, I visualized the elephant god Airavata with its seven trunks. More than any of the others this one was dense, the cement that anchored.

Dense matters needed to be consumed; meat or heavy protein, like Tofu or Azuki beans. Uneasiness grew within, compelling me to utter a word. The one inscribed within each of the petals before me.

"Lam," I whispered. Women's voices began echoing and chanting all around me. Some spoke in tongues, ones I'd known once. Ancient languages of Lemuria, Atlantis and Mu.

"Lam," I uttered louder.

Wind chimes clinked in the breeze, setting notes into vibrations that soothed notes in the soul. Flutes breathed in sequences and I turned, knowing I was no longer here. Pulled away to a time and place to begin my first lesson.

Stepping out of his room at the Enchantment resort bordering the mouth of Boynton Canyon Roger strolled down the pathway feeling bad for leaving his new wife behind but something kept prodding at him, especially after his encounters with the Maasaw dancer and the strange old man in the restroom that Beth swore blindly wasn't in there with him. He made love to her for over an hour, brought her to three gasping orgasms, *god that turns me on, hearing her moan as she cums,* before he finally released himself. It was something he learned in the Penthouse magazines he read as a teenager, how to control yourself from climaxing. There wasn't anything that enhanced his ego quite like driving your woman over the edge, again and again. Probably one of the reasons she adored him.

He walked along the forest service road and in minutes it seemed that he had left behind his wife and his world. Fading into the silence of the desert heat.

Alone.

Trust, just trust and overlook illusion. Oh, yeah, this is nuts. Yet, the nagging need to be here just kept calling. Like the visions in his dreams. Inspired by Bill and echoed further by the odd native man in the bathroom earlier in the day. *Who finds spiritual solace in a washroom?*

He stared up at the rock spire to his right, marking the entrance to the canyon. The guidebooks called it 'Kachina Woman'. From here, his friend Bill had told him, each step will take you deeper into yourself, deeper into another realm, deeper into your soul and deep into God and the Creator. Roger had laughed, saying Bill had probably smoked a big fat one like he'd been known to. He wasn't sure exactly what his friend had been trying to say, but it had intrigued him and deep inside he knew that calling had led him here. *Don't ask me why, I can't begin to explain, but I just know I must do this otherwise and if I didn't some massive part of my life will be for not.*

As he stood there Roger felt the knowing pull. Almost a mystical beckoning, tugging at him. Now he knew what powerful energies Bill had mentioned. Like a quiet voice whispering, the minute he and Barb had driven into town. Something almost disturbing, like the Maasaw dancer and the old man. Those hadn't helped matters, like at the airport when his 'get-the-hell-out-of-Dodge' sense was kicking in just before the metal detector went off.

Until recently, he really hadn't believed much in any of this spiritual mumbo-jumbo. If you can't prove it scientifically, it don't exist. Yet things were changing: he knew this somehow inside, couldn't explain it. A Spidey sense, as he called it from his comic book reading days, telling him something would go wrong. He rubbed at the bandaged wound on his side. Although it hadn't warned him about the metal. *Maybe I'd lost the force*, Roger laughed, *seduced by the dark side.*

The metal was wrapped in a box in his suitcase. *Should have thrown it away, but after all of the grief it caused, I couldn't. Will check with Bill about it. Maybe have it analyzed one day for what kind of metal it is.*

He never would have thought he'd be out by himself in a canyon in the middle of Arizona instead of snuggled up to his naked wife, who was still sweaty from her earlier excursions. All he knew was that for some reason it just felt right to lose his pondering mind and walk here. Brilliant ferrous basalt glowed shades of fire and gold in the sunset. He'd read in the guidebook that this particular canyon was both an electrical and a magnetic vortex. Standing here confirmed that, like on the edge of a whirlpool begging to dive into it. *Take the risk*, his inner voice whispered. *Only a risk to do what?*

Something had stirred. He had questions that needed answering in the last few days and this seemed as good a place as any. As he neared the head of the box canyon, Roger looked around him. All of this pulled at something, some sense of …

Déjà vu. He'd been here before, he was sure of it. Familiar, comforting, like he'd stepped down this path before. Maybe that's why he wanted to take this walk while Beth rested in the air-conditioned room.

Oh man, I'm either going bananas, had some rotten papaya juice or someone has slipped me some freaky drugs. What would make him think that? *I've never been here before, at least not in this lifetime.*

Each step sent a wash of familiarity, like walking through silken veils, all of his cares slipping away. He brushed against it earlier, whatever it was at the airport. Here he allowed the sheen and the static of the unknown to mellow him, cut him off from the rest of the world. Reaching inside to something gentle, restful. Everything becoming so dreamy, reality and all of its dilemmas slipping away. He'd done this before. This kind of karmic meditation, so familiar, like pulling down your new bed sheets for the first time over the familiarity of the place where you spent dreamtime. *How do I know I've done this before, yet never have been here? So familiar. The most mystical thing I've done before now has been watch Star Wars and Harry Potter.* Yet, there was something, a twinge every time he heard the Jedi Master's voice, Yoda. Like he'd been a student of some mystical school and had a teacher or was one as well.

He wanted to connect fully to the energy of this land. Without thinking he took off his shoes and socks, not caring about rocks, bugs or scorpions, he also put his cellphone into one of his shoes and shut it off. This was no place for disturbing electrical devices. The sand, still hot, sent waves of warmth up through him. The blistering heat of the late-day sun wasn't penetrating the canyons depths.

No, this was soothing, embracing. I need to trust, connect and go with the flow.

Grounding. Like the energy of the earth erupting up through his feet. He'd seen a movie once about how people that walk barefoot on the earth can heal many issues in their bodies.

That was it. This whole place was grounding him, pulling his worries away and settling him inside. He felt at peace here. *Was this what Bill had meant about this place? Maybe he wasn't so crazy after all.*

What had the native dancer said? Gateway walkers. The thought pulled at something from inside. Walking where? Gateway to what? Here? In this canyon?

Without thinking he sat down on the sand, crossed his legs under him and placed his palms face up on his knees. Like he'd seen in one of Beth's yoga tapes.

Like I'd done many times before. Roger shook his head. *I should be freaked out and was earlier. Not now. Now I only have questions as this is beginning to feel more and more normal. Like I've done this before in some other lifetime. Maybe I was a former Buddha monk or some apostle of Jesus. Well, that's if I believed in reincarnation.*

Unsure what to do, he simply trusted that by meditating, the answers, the reason he was here, would come. He closed his eyes and simply breathed, letting the song of his body settle in the harmony of the earth. *Seeing beyond the illusion. This should have felt foolish, but it just felt ... right.* So natural, yet he'd never done anything like this before. His friends would laugh their asses off if he told them right now what he was doing, which he wouldn't.

The sun shifted lower as he sat so still. Time either stilled or swept by.

Wind stirred, whistling in the canyon, curling around him. Shadows lengthened. A meditative state pulled him into ease, then like the drawing of blinds over ashen windows, the deep pull of sleep.

Tom sat before his computer desk. Last night's brunette had left before he'd got up.

Normally he would have phoned the number Daphne or Diane, whatever her name was, had left straight away to see if she wanted a repeat later tonight, but there was something more pressing to attend to and business always came first. At least he understood one thing, if he wasn't making the bucks, he couldn't afford this licentious style, nor the women or coke.

He picked up one of the holographic cards, flipped it open and instantly he was standing on a mountaintop. Tom turned, doing a 360-degree sweep. The effect was amazing, even to the point that he'd involuntarily raised his hand to cover his eyes from the sun's glare. The scene reminded him of the time his parents took him to the Colorado Rockies, but these slopes were even more lush in greenery and life. Trees swayed under a light breeze, water gurgled in mountain streams as they coursed away down the slopes. On another hillside below, he could make out a mama bear and her cub rolling around, obviously playing together. Tom sniffed the air, clean and invigorating, so full of life like he remembered smelling on that trip. A cry overhead.

He caught the site of a large American Bald Eagle circling, either looking for prey or enjoying the updrafts. Tom sank to his knees and touched the cool grass. "This is too real."

Wondering how long this could go on he sat down and relaxed, enjoying the view.

Finally, he glanced at his watch. An hour had passed. Still the eagle circled, and the bears played, with no obvious pattern to their movements revealed. But he sensed if he stayed here long enough they would repeat a set series of movements. He pulled a blade of grass free and, holding it between his lips, he blew on it, creating a shrill blast. Tom laughed, it was almost as if he was there, as a kid, on some mountaintop in the Rockies. He bit into it and the bitter taste of grass sprang down his throat. *Okay, not only visual, but somehow linked to the other five senses.* He ran his fingers over the damp grass, feeling the coolness and stared back at his wet fingers. *I have no idea what technology could pull this off, but this is astounding.*

"Okay, I wonder what the limits are of the scene." He stood up and took several steps down the slope. After about twenty steps the scene faded, and he was back in his bedroom.

A glance at his watch showed that indeed over an hour had passed away. "So, the time is real, but the scope of the pictures is limited. Good potential, but if these are only pictures of nature scenes then the only people that would buy them would be tree huggers."

As if in response to his query Tom opened a couple of cards and the next few stopped him in his tracks.

A couple naked in a dense forest. The woman straddling a man, her back arched in pleasure, he was obviously inside her. Both lost in the sheer pleasure of each other and nature.

Another of a couple in an elevator, the woman on her knees pleasuring a man. His hands trying to hold down the door close button. Moans reverberating in Tom's ears. Others of various groupings, even of two men in leather whipping each other. A bondage scene of two women; one a voluptuous blonde wearing a black and red leather corset. She was standing behind a chair, tied to which, by her hands, was a brunette wearing a sheer ice blue teddy. She was helpless. A whip dangled loosely from the blonde's hip. In all of them he was a voyeur, in the room with them but they couldn't see him.

"Wow! Now these are pictures I could stare at for a while." He felt the hardness creeping into his pants. "I can't sell the cute animal pictures for much ..." but he knew how much guys, and even women, would pay for holographs like these. One of the things he had invested in and was making a fortune at was pornographic websites. "Now these would make a fucking fortune." He wanted to grab a couple of beers, snort a line of coke and return to the pictures. But thought he'd better email the company first, let them know he was very interested.

He tried googling 'Unearthly Creatures' first, no signs of a webpage anywhere, or any hint of them on the internet. *Odd, very secretive.* Which could be good, if indeed very few people knew about this. Tom pulled up his E-trace software and punched in the coordinates from the package. He waited a minute while the program did its function, tracking down the location and owner of the website or email address he was after.

UnearthlyCreations@universe.com, 7872-7th Street, Los Angeles, CA.

Not much, but at least he had an address. Tom had visited LA a few times, searching Google Earth he soon came up with a rather innocuous skyscraper in downtown. In fact he had to go there on other business trip soon. Perhaps he might stop by to visit their offices as well. He grabbed his Apple Ipad and made a note to add that to his list of appointments.

"Okay, I'm interested, when can we meet?" He punched into the computer and sent his email off to the west coast.

Now to study the rest of the pictures. If any of the others could pull him in like the one he and the waitress at Manhattans Cafe viewed then he knew he had something unusual and cutting edge. Tom wasn't up to speed on the newest in holographic picture technology but if it checked out this thing looked more and more like a go. In fact, he had some friends in the movie special effects field in Hollywood that might shed some light on that thought. Tom buzzed off another email, to see if they were interested in also meeting next week. Research and 'know your territory' was always one of his underlying goals before signing any product. That and marketability and these pictures advertised the right way, could be huge.

I stumbled, falling head over heels over the furs I was dressed in. A crude wooden spear fell from my grasp. My heart raced, weariness seeped into every muscle screaming for rest. I was being chased and had been running all day, exhaustion slapped at every muscle. So tired, I thought the chakra lessons were supposed to increase my spiritual wellness. The only thing so far I'd learned was how well my lungs and legs worked.

Memory seeped into my head. I was a caveman, dodging from the hunter. My family and others had been killed by a pack of saber-tooth tigers. Some, like me, had escaped into the forest. Separated from the tribe, we were now easy pickings, a gruesome dinner. One of the large cats was tracking me. Intent on finishing me off, or just playing with me, I didn't know which. The thud of feline feet that haunted my every breath drove rational thought away, leaving only the slobbering fear that death hunted on four razor sharp paws and a set of equally long fangs.

I picked up my spear and looked around. I'd run into a canyon and before me a sheer stone wall stood. Behind me? The thump of paws as my hunter approached.

This was it. No escape. Shaking, I pressed myself against the cold stone, more to keep myself standing as sheer exhaustion sucked at me with its vampiric appetite, draining the use of my arms and legs; so tired. Seven-inch teeth glinted bone-white, coursing with the blood of my fellow tribesmen, as the big cat parted the bushes. I gripped the spear in rage, but no malice, no hate, stared at me from its eyes. It was merely doing what it must, what it was designed to do. To hunt and kill those weaker than itself. Just as every carnivore had been put here to do, it was about to cull the herd. Bring balance to the equation they called life. It was done chasing its food, teasing itself, now ready to feed, to eat. Its big wet tongue licked at the slavering lips.

I shook, my spear suddenly feeling flimsy. This great feline would take on the huge cave bears without fear. No survival here. I would die. Still, it was nature to try, to not give up. Struggle to survive. The saber-tooth charged and I yelled, my last instinct, screaming revenge as I raised the spear.

The big cat swatted the weapon aside in mid-leap, breaking it and then me like a twig, piercing my windpipe with its fangs. Blood, mine, splattered the rock. At the crunch of jaws I gurgled, staring at death through the killer's eyes. Nerves severed, jugular vein gushing my life fluid onto the soil, onto itself and myself, as it dragged my limp body off to dine in safety.

The sharp cry of a hawk overhead.

Roger opened his eyes: midnight blue sky stared back. He looked around but couldn't find the raptor that had broken his peace.

Memories of a tiger's savage cry reverberated in his mind, fading away.

Another cry and a glint from behind him. Maybe the bird was injured? He walked over to the stones peering around. No bird and no tiger. *I was still in Boynton Canyon, was I not? I'd fallen into some kind of meditative sleep after the walk and the great sex with my wife.*

He squinted, the source of the glint. Quartz. Glints of quartz crystals were everywhere; why hadn't he noticed it earlier? *Sparkling in the darkness?* Was it merely the changing angles of light as the sun sank?

Now what?

He examined the crystals. The scattered beams of light shifting, as he stared, into prisms of colors colliding and from those depths, a pattern, patterns? He closed his eyes, trusting what the old man had said. Patterns in his mind, leading him towards a darkening in the canyon wall. Darkening?

Could it be a cave? An entrance to somewhere? The truth whispered to his ears as Roger approached the dark area that looked more and more like a cave mouth. The quartz glinted all around like road markers.

How is this possible? He stood in the entrance, letting his eyes adjust to the partial darkness, focusing on a glow emanating from more crystals set into the rock walls, like light bulbs each turning on as he walked up to them.

He bent and shuffled along the tunnel. If so many people visited this canyon for meditation, why hadn't anyone reported this in the articles he read about the canyon?

After several minutes he was penetrating deep into the bowels of the Earth. There were no side channels, no way of getting lost. If the crystals went out, which somehow he knew they wouldn't, he'd be lost down here in the pitch blackness. *I have to trust they will light my way.*

At one point he heard an odd sound, put his ear to the light crystals and discerned a faint purring, almost as if they were singing. Soothing and reassuring. He knew it was safe to continue. *The crystals have sensed my presence and approve. What a crazy thing to think.*

Just ahead the light brightened and he entered a large cavernous opening, probably two hundred feet across. He peered up into the darkness, didn't know how high. Had he gone down this far before? It didn't seem like it.

All around him crystals; from small finger sized red and emerald greens, to larger, nearly the length of his arm in pale jean washed blues and majestic, royal purples hummed and glowed. In the center were what looked like markings on the dusty floor. Roger stepped back, careful to not disturb the rubbings, not knowing if they meant anything, but intuitively afraid he'd destroy a thousand, thousand years of knowing if he did.

Circles upon overlapping circles.

The humming was loudest here. Reminding him of a car's engine, idling. Waiting to be revved. Only how do you fire up a crystal? Is this what the Maasaw meant?

A gateway walker. *Am I in a gateway now? A corridor out of this world?*

He was supposed to do what? Rearrange the crystals, wake up the energy flow, like undamming a river? *It was wasn't it? How do I know that these crystals are out of alignment?*

A voice from deep within, replied.

It was you who did this, you who will know, when the time comes, what to do.

Roger yawned and as his lips stuck to each other, he realized how thirsty his body was. He hadn't anticipated being out for so long and foolishly had not brought water. But the cave was so full of peaceful energy that he was reluctant to leave. He took a last glance around, *I'll be back. I trust inside, that I don't know what to do here yet, but that this room is like a TV set unplugged.*

He closed his eyes, tilted back his head and everything swam around him. Roger felt consciousness pull away from him. He slumped forward and lurched himself awake before falling on his face. *What just happened?* He glared around and found himself in the lotus position he'd adopted earlier before he discovered the chamber. *I haven't moved from this place? Have I?*

What?

He must have fallen asleep; *it was all just some sort of lucid dream?*

He put on his shoes and socks and walked over to the rocks he'd studied earlier. In the increasing darkness, no crystals glinted. The whole wall of the canyon was shadowed. *Obviously no cave either. Just a mad dream. One of many I've had lately.*

A howl jolted him and another joining the first, sounding closer.

Time to go. Before I become coyote or wolf road stew.

He hurried back to the resort, stopping only to stare up at the spire of the Kachina Woman. The crystal cave had seemed so real. And then it hit him. The cave was indeed humming, idling like an engine in a vehicle with a manual transmission. This wasn't a dream or some sort of water-deprived delusion. This was real and he had to return. No, he **would** return and do something there, of that he was certain. But what?

A chorus of howls shattered the darkness. Coyotes? Or wolves? Something about dogs and being chased sent a shiver down his back. Ancient fears from his childhood.

He hurried back, grabbing an old tree limb, just in case.

When the cosmos says to adios, it means it. I guess, Roger smirked as he hoofed it back.

Doorways? Gateways?

The old man and the horrid dancer had said.

Gateway walkers ... hadn't I just walked through a gateway in my dreams to someplace I've been before? Someplace I've never experienced. Some lifespan I've never lived or had I yet?

I picked up the spear-shaped stick that had been a piece of furniture until the bombs began falling, and wedged it into the door. The thud of explosions, rocket-fire, bombs falling, reverberated in the background. The Germans had surprised my people and had attacked. Now they were before the very gates of Leningrad.

As I turned from the doorway a mirror caught me in its sight. Sixteen and toting a gun, a soldier, raised to be a killer. How glorious the communist teachings were, an honor to fight for the Motherland. The Motherland, my mother, I only wanted to know if my mother was still alive. If she could hold me, like she did when I was six. Summers of lazy days on the farm, playing with my sister, being tucked in at night. Gone, all gone. I clenched the only comfort I knew now, the cold caress of my gun's muzzle.

Only now the snow was falling, or was it soot and debris, and the thump of boots in the hallway. Real soldiers bearing sub-machine guns and the gray uniforms of the swastika, the former Buddhist symbol of the wheel of life stolen. I knew this, not from this lifetime, but from another. Now the war engine of destruction, of Aryan invincibility. The wheel that crushed all who opposed. No, I wouldn't give up. I cocked my single-shot rifle and waited. Boots, scurrying like rats, now in the hallway. Gunshots, screams, gurgled gasps. Sweat poured from my brow.

A kick sent splinters of shattered spear flying. Bullets ripped. I aimed as the door exploded inward, wishing I were shooting groundhogs on our farm on peaceful days in summers past. My bullet punches square between the eyes of the cold hearted soldier's stare. His face explodes in red mist and I cheer inside at ending the life of another human being as I reload the cumbersome rifle. The intruder falls in a heap.

Another appears behind him, hot death stinging a rain of acrid gunpowder. Soon winter would be here, freezing everything, even them. But not soon enough, not tonight, as a dozen points of lead mushroomed inside, scattering my flesh like confetti into the floral nursery wallpaper behind me. I fell back, shattering a crib that could have been mine, in a mist of red.

That night, after he'd returned, he woke her up and they made love again. He didn't tell Beth about his experience in the canyon, other than he went for a walk. As Roger fell asleep he lay dreaming. Thoughts of traveling through space, images of suns, double suns and triple suns. A world with four moons and a ring of rock sweeping overhead. An ache sounded within, an ache for a place.

I once belonged.

He awoke with a start. His encounters yesterday with the eerie native dancer and the elderly native shaman had been no coincidence. Changes had begun a progression of something that had been there all this time. Only now something inside had shifted and was allowing this pathway to open. It too had been there all the while, just waiting for the tread of feet to warm its stones and disturb the dust.

Already the dream was slipping away ... he really should write it down. A familiarity struck him, echoes of former lives, of a place once called home.

Night mist swirls around. It would hide my escape with the dawn. My dark skin blended into the murky waters of the Derwent River. The dreamtime of my people was ending, now to be renamed; Tasmania, land of new hope. But only for the white-skinned. Not for my kind, even though we'd dwelt here for tens of thousands of years. Our hope was vanishing.

The two Amerjigs stood on the bank of the Derwent. Caverns just behind them were adorned with pictures depicting all my ancestry, overlain by others and others still, this I knew. The trials, the important times, the good things, the dreamtimes. After I died, these would become eroding pigments, to be stared at, wondered and studied by ignorant others that know nothing of us. Imbeciles trying to decipher gibberish.

"Come on Jim, I've skinned these two abo's. I reckon we'll drink good for the next couple weeks."

"Shh. Don't you smell that stink? Think there's one we missed, in the water. Still too early." Jim stared into the sky at the sun beginning to rise behind the mountains.

I cursed. That one had good hunter sense, like mine. He knew what was there when nothing could be seen, a common trait of my people. He can sense what there is not to be seen.

"Another? Hey, maybe we'd have enough then for a spot of fun with one of the Sheilas back in Hobart. What d'ya say?"

"I say he's watching us. Crazy abo's, they can talk to each other in their heads, I tell you."

"You're nuts."

"Can't say if that's the truth, but I tortured one once for days and he told me so, before I cut out his tongue." Jim rubbed the dried appendage dangling from the rawhide around his neck.

"Here we go again, mate. You're as bananas as the savages. Thinking its tongue gives you special powers like some ... what d'ya call it? In the East Indies. Oh yeah, voodoo charm."

"You forget, I lived up in the Vancouver Island colony for a while. Their shamans would battle certain animals and wear their tongues around their necks so as to control their powers. Don't forget how many it's led us to. We took more skins than all the other bounty hunters combined, and right now it's telling me there's one more alive in this river." Jim held the talisman in one hand and stared out into the water. "Yes sir, right now he's fearing us, hating us. Dangerous as a cornered croc."

"You scare me with that hokey-pokey stuff. Stick to the good book, that's what I've been raised on. The good Lord will never steer you

wrong. Besides, what's so dangerous about them? We got lead on our side, they got spears and those crazy throwing sticks."

"Boomerangs they're called, and they can take down a 'roo from 'alf a mile."

I rose from my sinkhole, knowing the mist would dissipate and leave me visible from the riverbank. I cranked back my arm and pitched the boomerang. That dumb mutant would never defile another body of my people. Kill only for food and never for revenge. But the other one, the smart one, was right. There were no others left on this dreamtime and I had the right to claim a few in revenge for all of us they'd slaughtered.

Jim dove as soon as he heard the swish.

"What's that?" Bill turned, his last words faded away to the boomerang's hiss, ceasing completely when its edge clove into his skull. He pitched forward, falling into the murdered corpses.

Shots rang out. Pain ripped into my body as I ducked back under the water. Blood gushed from my throwing arm, staining the water with red. The arm was useless now. My people always said revenge never paid. Maybe so but for once if I was the last of my kind I would take at least one soul with me testament to a warrior's pride.

"Bloody hell. Knew there was at least one savage left in this province. But probably no more, I think." Jim approached the river's edge. "Yup. I think you're the very last one, aren't you?"

He was right, dreamtime was over and now there was no one to sing me away on my journey back home. Alone. I smiled. At least there would be one white-skinned one to ease my passage.

I sank to the bottom and crossed my legs, found a couple of rocks and propped them over me as best as I could. I waited, water humming in my ears. The earth singing to me of the passage of my kind. I smiled. Something to sing me home, until the pressure got too great to hold my breath. No, this one would not get me. I would survive to journey to the real world. He would not claim my scalp.

"Damn crazy savage." Jim stared down into the sinkhole. The stream of red rising as the sun crested the hills and the waters took *it away to the ocean. "He's down there and I can't get to him. Knew I shoulda took up swimming in Sunday school."*

The large burst of bubbles surfaced; the body did not. "Probably lashed himself to a rock or something. Crazy bugger." Jim ripped the necklace from his throat and threw it into the water. "Don't need you now, mate. There's none of them left." He studied the hides. "Well, since there's double the money for me, might as well get myself a good slow Sheila and some fast whiskey."

The tongue talisman settled into my lap as the last gasp of air left me and I rose with it from my body, releasing my hand from the tile in the pyramid.

I turned over in my sleep in my bed in Sedona.

A whisper from the dark. "Your first lesson has ended." I could see the Hathor being with a long thin smile.

God I wanted to punch him!

Chapter Five

Roger woke with a start as lightning light up the room. He counted the seconds, like he'd done ever since he'd been a kid.

"Eight, nine, te- -" Thunder crashed all around. A full blown summer storm. He loved these but they didn't get many out here on the West coast, not like the prairies where, as a child, he sat on his balcony and watched the whole world go crazy in the fireworks nature displayed. Life on the coast seemed a lot tamer weather wise, except for the eternal depressing gray skies in the winter. *Well, still better than 40 below zero, ten months of winter and two of bad slush.*

"Damn! I think I left Sparky outside," he muttered. Roger slipped out from under the warm security of his blankets, careful not to disturb Beth as the weirdly bizarre dream left him. *Something about a Spook-like teacher, being eaten by tigers, shot by soldiers and being drowned in Australia. I gotta quit eating late at night. Beth's right, gives you nightmares. Only it didn't feel like a nightmare.* It felt like some kind of strange psychic journey he'd started on. Dreams that haunted his mind as he fell asleep. *This began when they cut that damn piece of metal out of me.* Realizations hit him.

He thought about it a moment as he tiptoed around the bedroom. Although why he bothered to tip toe around he wasn't sure. *She could sleep through a stampede of elephants on crutches. Why do I get the impression those dreams were more like lessons?*

Freaky ones, but lessons indeed.

Rain and trees thrashed about outside and gusts of wind slapped the house, as thunder cracked and lightning sang its electric harsh voice. Roger stared at her, incredulous that she continued to sleep away like Dracula snuggled in his cozy coffin oblivious to the world rocking and rolling outside. Hail hammered at the windows in a bizarre tinging melody with no rhyme or reason.

The calling of chaos. Words spoken by my teacher. *Why do I get the feeling that metal triggered this, or is that co-incidence as well?* He remembered his hands touching the stone in the pyramid at the beginning of his first lesson and the words of the tall being behind him. "There is no co-incidence."

Although I guess that's a good thing, gave me time to check out Boynton Canyon in Arizona. I swear that woman never even rolled over in her sleep that night.

They'd just got back two nights ago. Another lightning bolt lit up the room for a moment. "Ah, my slippers" he said, taking advantage of the brilliance. Roger slipped them on and grabbed his bathrobe, slamming his toe into the edge of the dresser. "Fuc..." He began to swear and finished cursing into his hand as he clapped it over his mouth. Muttering obscenities he limped down the hallway in the semi darkness, his guts were telling him this wasn't going to be a simple matter.

Sparky was an integral part of their family. Beth had two kids, Jen and Mark, from a previous relationship. He had a dog, Sparky, thirty-five in human years. Her two kids loved dearly, but Beth called him one of the punter breed of dogs. She obviously more of a cat lover. "A perfect blended family," Roger laughed every time Sparky would haul off one of her slippers for a chew session and Beth chased him down. Dogs knew when someone didn't like them, Roger would tell Beth. After all, he never chewed his master's slippers.

"That's because you never wash them and they stink. The dog isn't stupid." She replied.

Opening the backdoor a crack icy rain and hail blasted him before he could holler his dog's name. Roger closed the door, sputtered and reopened it. This was definitely not looking to be a simple matter.

Squinting his eyes tightly he inhaled deeply, another rush of rain laced with hail peppered his forehead. He looked around, "Sparky!" He bellowed twice, not caring if the whole neighborhood woke up at this point, fully expecting to see his slipper-chewing companion's grateful face.

"Damn. I guess that warm bed is just going to have to wait."

Roger trudged through his house. Threw on his bright yellow raincoat complete with seafarer's cap and stomped to the backdoor accompanied only by the squeak of the rubber raincoat. Surprisingly no one had woken up yet. Ready to face the elements he opened the door again.

Same ritual; rain, hail in face, no dog.

"I should leave that mangy newspaper shitter outside. It would serve him right." He thought of the times Sparky would dump all over his work papers instead of the newsprint when he was house training him. "I shoulda trained you to read English." Roger remembered saying to Sparky, as he tried drying his documents off with a hair dryer. "Newspaper, work-papers. See the difference. Hey, let's go throw a ball." Sparky would just look at him with a stupid no comprendo look on his face, bark twice and pant. The face of his dog as a puppy swam in front of him and all the times he'd fallen asleep by the TV with his dog beside him, head in his lap. His best friend before Beth came along.

Damn! I hate having a conscience. I'm too nice for my own good. Wind whistled all around him as he pulled the rain-slicker tight against his head. Clicking on the flashlight he scoured the area. *I just know I'll run into the aunt of all aliens or Count Vladimer's uncle hungry for a late night snack, namely me. I can see the headlines now. Remains of man found, DNA tests confirm the one square millimeter remains were indeed of Roger Harrison found among bits of yellow rubber while out searching for his dog. Dog Found Safe in Neighbor's House. Neighbor suing deceased man's estate for soiled newspapers.*

"Sparky," he growled.

Nothing. But rain peppering him.

Roger fumed as he sloughed across the back alley through mud puddles to Sparky's haunts. Much to the chagrin of his neighbors, that dog never seemed to want to do his thing in his own yard?

He walked to the end of the block.

Again, nothing.

There was one more place he knew the dog would sometimes go. Beside two empty lots, stood Mrs. Miller's old place. Sparky sometimes hung out there, mainly because the elderly, nearly deaf, woman would feed him scraps and bones. Roger felt cold rain trickle down his back, the dastardly substance somehow managing to find a way under the raincoat.

Now he was getting upset. "Sparky!" A movement just past the house caught his attention. Roger walked past the old abandoned garage and looked under the step. "Funny, there's a light on in that garage." He knew Mrs. Miller's husband had died five years ago and thought she'd not used the garage since. Sure enough there was his sock-eating buddy, chewing on a bone about twice the size of the dog. Safe and dry under the step. "You got room under that step for company?" He asked Sparky.

Lightning flashed again.

"Holy, where'd Mrs. Miller get a bone that large?" Sparky panted and barked twice, obviously happy to see his master as he ran up to Roger. "You know for a little dog, you sure are a major pain. Come on boy, let's go home." Sparky barked again and returned licking at his bone. He wasn't about to leave such a prize snack behind. "Okay, I'll take it with us. I'm too bloody nice to you." Roger crawled under the step giving the bone a yank, "this thing must weigh twenty pounds, about ten more then you, wet or dry. Even if you ate your doggy Wheaties you'd never be able to drag this thing. How'd you get it here?" He groaned, dragging bone and grateful-licking-his-hand dog along the crawlspace. "We'll have to thank Mrs. Miller later for this. Although right about now I should give her a piece of my mind for lack of sleep, freezing my butt off and wet clothing. Grrrr."

Lightning flared up again, revealing what looked like a small trapdoor hanging loose, flapping under the rear of the garage. "Unless you've been smuggling them out." Roger hoisted the bone onto his shoulder and Sparky under his other arm.

As thunder began its slow rumbling build-up, another flash of lightning, the strongest so far, lit up the night. Out of the corner of his eye Roger caught a movement; a shadow silhouetted against the side of the building. Then it was gone. A vision of platinum hair spinning away. Her? The woman that haunted some of his dreams and on occasion he swore he'd spot in a crowd and at a second glance she'd be gone like some vanishing act set up by a magician.

As Roger walked along the length of the garage another brilliant flash tore into the ground just as he looked up into its darkened window, illuminating the entire area. What was that? Roger stared at the window but saw nothing in the dark. A sudden feeling of being watched and of trouble pulled at him. "Time to go, buddy." He suddenly didn't like standing beside the building, nor staring into the dark window. *Trouble with a big R, I'm sensing and I've learned to trust my intuition over the years. Or usually, should have listened to it at the airport.*

Shadowy figures in the garage. Stuffed animals, perhaps? Hadn't her late husband been a taxidermist? Maybe she hadn't gotten rid of his work? Eerie.

Lightning exploded overhead. He caught her reflection, again, against the side of the garage. In crowds he'd sometimes see her, disguised, watching him, protecting him in dangerous situations?

He'd seen her more often as a reckless teenager. Roger was sure she'd even saved his life, once. Why here? Why tonight? It had been a long time since he'd seen her, or thought he'd seen her. Had it been because of what he'd seen briefly in the window of the garage? She usually showed up when there was danger to him. *My guardian angel, that everyone I ever mentioned it too thought I was bonkers.*

Although I haven't seen a glimpse of her in many years. Not even at the damn airport. Funny that, when I could have used her the most.

"Come on Sparky, it's time to go home." Roger bent his head trying to let the cap of his raincoat deflect most of the rain. He walked down the alley, his dog bundled in one arm, the large bone now under the other. "Yup, it's sure been a strange one," he muttered, juggling the dog and the bone as he opened the door. Roger set the bone and Sparky down. "Now don't move while I get a towel to dry you off." Sparky ran over to the bone and flopped beside it, licking it, like he'd never heard Roger. "Well it's obvious I just wasted my breath. All this trouble over one lousy bone." Only it wasn't just about a bone, was it? Sparky old boy. Something else was going on here. Something that would attract what he named many years ago as his guardian angel.

So why here and why now?

We stood on a mountain escarpment overlooking a high plain. Below us dozens of old stone buildings. Greenery falling away on steep, once terraced, slopes into mist rising. Machu Picchu?

Perhaps, I wasn't sure as a single step covered hundreds of feet in dizzying fashion. We tread on cobblestones, echoing of age and antiquity, as cold to the touch as the still mountain slopes shivering up to the deep blue sky all around us. Air, nearly devoid of oxygen, pulled at my breath. Entering the sacred city, beams of light danced between the streets and the buildings.

Seamless walls of precision fit gargantuan blocks hide not even a cranny to slip paper money between them. I study the blocks as we walk by, cut with so many sides I lose count, and gasp for breath. My body hungers for more than the scant traces of oxygen here. How? Could they build in these dizzying heights? I surmise. How?

Only this town isn't deserted. What I thought at first were beams of light dancing I realized now were spirit-like beings with gossamer wings. When they land invisible bodies reappear as they touch earth. Expanding wings caught the light and glowing like firebugs, they take off and flit about again. Nearly invisible.

Overhead three suns glow, each one dim, but together they cast about the same brilliance as ours. So full of joy, the odd sprite, for lack of another term, smiling always smiling, would glance our way.

"Content lot, aren't they?" I finally spoke.

"Very. Your legends of pixies and fairies sprang from these folks. They still visit, but not as often as they used to."

"Why not?"

"That will be up to you to repair."

"Repair?"

"No more said, we go to the lowlands, now."

"We're not on Earth are we?" I asked as we walked.

"No. Your sun would be rising into view around midnight." As it spoke the sky darkened for a moment. I gasped and looked up into the sea of stars. There were millions, but they looked so unfamiliar.

"Where?" I asked. "All I see are st..."

"In that grouping of seven stars, which the dwellers of this world call Gaymede, the seeder." It pointed over my shoulder.

As I gaped the night sky ebbed and we returned to daylight. It continued to walk. I stumbled along in shock.

Another step, we left the town and began down a pathway dug by the tread of feet over a millennia. I stopped, listening to the echoes of water drops formed from the moisture saturated air dripping from branch to branch. I caught a glimpse of something flashing and noticed another smaller trail. "Wait."

The Hathor smiled, "go ahead, we have time."

"I guess we do, in the fourth dimension." I laughed, time truly folded over here in meaningless rapport.

I stepped down the trail, through a ring of trees and stood in a clearing. It was well kept. In the center was a fair sized area of white sand carefully raked and polished, like a Japanese Zen garden. A single monolith stood in the center, concentric raked circles radiated from it. Order complete order derived from the chaos of nature all around us.

"Only to nature, this is complete chaos." He spoke. "It all depends on viewpoint."

I walked around the outside perimeter of the garden, realizing that something was scrawled into the surface of the rock. Writing, it looked like writing, only it was so hard to see, as water was slowly dripping down its sides and disappearing into the ground.

The Hathor stood quietly. I asked it, with my mind, "is that writing?"

It didn't answer my question, instead merely said "trust, you simply must trust."

I looked round, there were no spirit beings to ask. I took off my sandals and stepped into the sand, which was surprisingly warm. I could hear the trickles of water now and as I stepped closer the sound of water increased until it sound like a stream. I took another step forward, past a ring of carefully tended sand, and the stream grew in strength, water flowing. I took another step. The stream wound over rocks, sounding stronger, yet still only bare trickles fell down the surface of the boulder.

As I stepped closer, water cascaded into my ears until it became a wall of white noise. A mighty river pounding down a steep mountain valley.

I turned and stared behind me, no footsteps were to be seen, as if the water in waves of vibrations corrected my passage. Either that or I simply couldn't see the water flowing all around me. Water flows in the path of least resistance, growing until it gains enough strength to cut mighty canyons. I turned back to the monolithic rock and noticed for the first time six lotus petals inscribed in a pattern around a circle. I knew where I was.

"This is the garden of Svadhisthana, the second chakra. Water rules here." The Hathor spoke over the thunder of cascading waters. "Liquidity. Energy is never static, like the ocean it ebbs and flows in a constant state of flux."

I squinted closer, sacred symbols were written on each petal. Two figures sat cross-legged, one a man and the other a woman. Each held objects and as I stared I could feel the heat from inside my lower abdomen. Hunger and passion.

"It is also the sexual chakra, all desire, all energy erupts from here. Yin and Yang, each part of the whole, each incomplete without the other. The petals surround the moon. The moon instills emotions on all who gaze at it. The moon pulls on the waters, tides form and energy releases. The circle also represents the womb, this chakra is very feminine as the seed of life springs from passion. All desire, all movement, begins here."

Was it me? Heat building as the Hathor talked. Intense, burning arousal. I felt his words blurring away, I could only feel the passion erupting. Hear the urge, tremble in the want. Embarrassed, I turned away, trying to hide my hardness.

"Good Day, Mr. Bradley," the agent said, as Tom slid into his seat at the restaurant. Tom had been running a few minutes late. Something he didn't want to do for this meeting.

"Look, I'm sorry, I got carried away at the office with some pressing business and…"

"Don't bother explaining Mr. Bradley, you are here and that is what is important," the rather attractive female client said.

Tom smiled. He liked the sound of her voice, musical in tone. "Your accent is intriguing. Are you from Sweden?" he asked, guessing from her striking natural looking platinum hair. No tell-tale roots. Yet her face held the flawless petite features of an oriental girl, except for her eyes which had the epicanthic fold unlike true Orientals. *Well baring any operations, that is.*

"Actually, consider me from the East, the very far East. However, we have business to attend to." She glanced at her watch quickly.

Her external sensors were beginning to alert her of approaching dangers.

"Okay, right. I was just getting in a little small talk." She was obviously a business first, pleasure later type of woman, thought Tom. "So, as you can judge by my email I'm interested in your holographic pictures. This must be a new type of process you're using. They do seem rather unique." They were, the boys he emailed last night hadn't heard of anything like this, they wanted to see a copy and try to figure out how the process worked. If they were interested and puzzled this was something new and cutting edge, maybe made by some young whiz kids. The image of a cash register and dollar signs sprung before his eyes.

"That I am not privileged to talk about. I am only an agent for the people I represent." She smiled coolly at him. "As you can understand, my clients will not divulge anything to do with the cutting edge processes involved in the making of these pictures. Patent rights and other legal issues."

God, this woman is not only gorgeous but hard as nails, Tom thought. He glanced at her left hand as she raised her glass of water to take a sip. Even better, she had no ring.

The pictures, like I said, are unique. I feel that I can market them with the potential for very good sales for your client. Now normally I would have put together something of a package to show you how I might present these pictures to the public, but with the short time-frame I didn't have that luxury, nor am I sure just what approach to use. I can do this in a few days and then we could proceed from there if you like." Tom said with a straight face, he didn't want to look too eager. *She said Far East, Japanese or there were a lot of upstart Chinese and Thai companies coming on line lately. But she looked more Swedish than anything.*

"Well, then, I think that we can perhaps work something out. I don't think a presentation will be necessary, my clients would prefer to remain invisible at this time. However, they will supply the product as you see it. The marketing and packaging are yours to handle."

"I do my own packaging, advertising and target marketing?"

"Yes."

"And what is the profit margin in this?"

She smiled for the first time. "I've a pricing sheet attached to this new package of pictures. My client is more interested in getting his product out there then making a huge profit. I think you'll find their selling price and wholesale price quite attractive." Her sensors were going off again. "Now, I have to rush myself for another meeting."

That wasn't the only thing Tom found attractive. Her voice was like music. Very arousing.

"Then I think he has a tentative deal and you have your marketing man." Tom rose and extended his hand. "I can have a package put together of the final product to show you in two months." Two months was really pushing it, he knew, but this was something that he had to get on quick, before someone else did. He had no idea if anyone else was being asked to look at marketing these products. "Am I to understand I'm under an exclusivity contract?"

"Two months is acceptable. After that, no guarantees." She rose and shook his hand. "Some of these new pictures you'll find are newer more refined versions of the ones you've already viewed. My contact number and email are on the business card inside." She glanced quickly at her watch again. The screen blinking, obviously something else was on her agenda. "I'm ah, running severely late for another appointment."

Tom stared at the package and the number scrawled on it. "Is this your personal access number?"

"Yes."

"Can I call you then on a more personal matter?"

"How personal are we talking?"

"How about dinner?" He was being direct, he knew, but it was his usual approach when dealing with attractive women. Ask for what you want, sometimes he'd get slapped, sometimes he'd get lucky.

Tom really hoped she'd be one of the lucky ones. Her handshake sent shivers through him with its warmth and strength. She obviously worked out. Good. He was in the mood for an aggressive woman, especially after viewing those pictures of the woman tying her man to the bedpost the other night.

"No." She picked up her coat, briefcase and smiled. "Actually, yes you can. I haven't been with a male, a man, for quite a while. A night out would be rather delicious." She purred and walked away. "Sorry something urgent has come up and I've got to get going."

Tom tried not to show that he was shocked by her response and watched the sway of her hips as she walked away, feeling the blood drain from most of his anatomy into another section.

"Ah wait, I don't even know your name." He yelled across the restaurant.

She turned as she opened the door to leave. "Sherida, it's on the card inside." And vanished into the outside world.

His eyes puffy, Roger sipped at his morning coffee, needing its kick-start to the heart more this morning than most. "Last night was just too much," he muttered.

"What was all that commotion about last night?" Beth said above the gut growling smells of bacon and eggs frying.

"What is the million dollar question, more like how? How you managed to sleep through last night in one of the worst thunderstorms I've seen out here."

"It was thundering last night?" *And the dreams after were just too much.*

That woman could sleep through an Iron Maiden concert in her backyard, with Eddie their large skeleton insignia dangling from her clothesline, Roger thought. "Ah yeah, a major one and

I made the mistake of trying to find our dog out there in the downpour."

"Oh, did you get wet?"

"Thanks for the concern, it was pissing dogs, cats, large furry rodents and the occasional hippo, no I stayed very dry, thank you. As for Sparky, I found him over at Mrs. Miller's."

"Just hang on Rog. Gotta get the kids up." Beth left him alone to fume into his cooling coffee.

Roger stared down at the headlines in the morning paper. 'Drug War Erupts Downtown. Four Found Shot In Bedroom'. "Wow this town is getting scary, drug shootouts in hotels. Mind you, every third rental property is getting busted for being a grow-op."

"What in the ... Roger do you know anything about this?" Beth yelled from the hallway.

Roger looked up from his paper, wishing they had some Tylenol right about now, his head throbbing. He wanted to say, "What part of my earlier conversation didn't you hear about Sparky and his large bone last night," but knew out of respect for wanting any sex in the next month or so, he didn't. "If your 'what in the ...' refers to that bone laying by the door step, yes, I know about it." He put down his paper and shuffled over to the coffee pot.

"So what are you going to do with that overgrown dinosaur bone? How about tossing it outside before one of our kids trips over it and breaks their necks?" She said, as she came around the corner.

"What did you say?"

"I said take this bone outside. It's in my way. I'm trying to cook breakfast here, the kids are getting up and I gotta go to work."

"No, you called it a dinosaur bone." Well it was big enough to be one, but why would Mrs. Miller have it in her garage and as he glanced down at it realized there were still bits of what looked like fresh flesh attached. *Odd, if her hubby died five years ago this should be dried meat.*

"I don't care what I called it, Rog. I was joking. Just get it out of here."

"Right. Check, got it. Memory forever, message received, zero distortion." He smiled and stumbled to the door. She was right about one thing, it was big enough to be a dinosaur bone. With a grunt he hefted it, swearing it'd swelled double its weight overnight. His angel, he'd forgotten to tell Beth he'd seen her last night. Only how do you mention to your wife that you've a beautiful blonde woman haunting you and considering their wacky honeymoon, probably better mentioned another time when lots of wine is involved. From what he knew of Beth, she wouldn't take this lightly, being very jealous, especially of 'those younger blonde bitches' as she so politely put it.

Sparky came running out from somewhere in the backyard. He'd been chewing on another bone, a smaller version of the one Roger placed a couple of feet from the back entrance. Roger looked around the yard. There were at least two other partly chewed remains of bones scattered in his yard. "Wow. Its been awhile since I've been in the backyard, obviously." He glanced at all of the bones. *All of these look like they've been stripped of meat only recently. Is our sweet elder a psycho killer?* In fact one had some staining from blood oozing out of its broken end that Sparky had been chewing on.

He walked back into the house. "I think I'm going to talk to Mrs. Miller and see if I can board up that trapdoor before our dog drags a whole carcass over here."

"He's got another bone?"

"Several. I found him under her garage chewing on the one I tossed outside. I did see what looked like a trapdoor half open in Mrs. Millers place. I'll bet he's getting them from there."

"That's ridiculous. What would an old lady be doing with a large animal in her garage?"

"Well, I don't rightly know, last I knew the rats haven't evolved into four foot zombie-like creatures, which I'm sure we'll see on TV in some new horror grade B flick, I could barely lift it. But he couldn't haul the bone I got last night this far, probably why he stayed under the garage. So it must have come from there. Don't forget her husband was a taxidermist."

"Yeah, but he died a few years ago and it doesn't make any sense, since that bone had fresh, ugh, meat on it and traces of blood. You do whatever you want, but if that animal is several years old my may want to make sure he's had all of his shots. He could get some kind of food poisoning or venereal disease."

"You can't get VD from eating old dog bones, Mad Cow Disease, could be cow bones, maybe."

"Whatever, just make sure the bones get picked up before the kids cut the grass this weekend, and don't forget you promised to take them to the Natural History Museum on Friday for school. Your eggs are just about done, can you watch them?"

Beth gave him a peck on his cheek and licked at his ear. She squeezed his buns as she walked by.

"Hey, what was that for?"

"That was for a most delicious job well done last night." She smiled, rolling her eyes and wiggling her hips as she walked down the hallway.

He'd forgotten about the lengthy lovemaking session they had after the kids had been put to bed. She was the first multi-orgasmic woman he'd ever had and Man, did she do something to his ego and his hunger. "Well, I can make it a repeat performance tonight."

"You're on." Beth smiled lewdly. "I do like encores."

Sherida cringed quickening her pace as she rounded the corner from the restaurant, wanting to wash her hand of Tom's sliminess after walking out. *Some human males are revolting and only think of one thing. Why do I get the feeling I'm wasting my time in seeing if he is the One we want. But the training did say ignore personal bias and stay neutral.*

Remember the first protocol. Never put her emotional judgments in the way of the process. He would do that himself, she knew. After all what was the expression they used here, 'Only the good die young and nice guys finish last'. The council didn't care who or how the codes were cracked as long as someone did it. *Even if he's a disgusting pig.* It was up to him to find the goodness in his soul, no one else. *All part of the process and not all saints are blessed.* She remembered the words during her lessons.

Right now she had her own problems as her built-in senses warning her of approaching danger were going off again. She was being scanned and followed and needed to distance herself from Tom. Not sure if they wanted her or her contacts. But after the other night, most likely her. The report she read of the kids in Florida, had been mysteriously killed by a mysterious creature and from the description it sounded Dractarian. Roger was safe, for now and beginning his process of discovery.

So far she'd been unable to contact Lyra, her home world and that had never happened before. Sherida frowned, she'd escaped the attack in her hotel room, but it appeared now that whoever was after her could track her as well. Someone or something was out to get her, so what about the other angels? There was no way of contacting them or was there? Only right now she had bigger problems, someone was obviously tracking her via her equipment and three separate signals were closing fast on her location.

She turned another corner and ran in the opposite direction into a alley, glancing at her wrist the targets changed direction also. How they were tracking her she'd have figure out later, but they were, that was obvious.

Ducking down a second alley, that was just wide enough to get two vehicles in side by side, she heard deep-hearted growl of Harleys approaching. Their method of transportation. Here she'd make her stand without alerting the public and hopefully human authorities.

In a blink her disguise vanished as she transformed into her black skin-tight battle outfit. From the other end of the alley several more bikers rumbled around the corner. Where'd they come from? Those she hadn't detected. This was very disturbing, her senses had failed to detect those ones.

One of the bikers pressed a button, everything beyond the ends of the alley went hazy. They had access to Lyran technology, this battle would be undetected by the humans and worse, Sherida was trapped in the middle.

Well, she had a few tricks up her sleeve. With the speed of her legs augmented as much as biochemical science would allow, she'd take the battle to them.

Two of the bikers reached for their holstered guns. Sherida covered the hundred foot distance in a blink. Two cracks rang out.

The third man, slower than the others, never had time to react as she slammed into his chest, crushing his chest cavity. A backflip, one's neck she snapped and the other she sent careening into a brick wall.

"Fuck, get the bitch," yelled one of the other three from the opposite side of the alley. The heavy growl of two Harleys under full throttle echoed off the concrete walls, deafening in the narrow confines of the alley. Sherida squinted, shutting down much of her auditory senses, trying to block out the rumble distorting all sense of whereabouts. It was the one's that eluded her danger sense she wanted.

The two closer bikers beside her stirred and one reached to free his gun. With a savage kick she sent his arm sprawling behind his back and vaulted over the bike. Someone fired a shot. Sherida sidestepped the bullet, disorientated by the reverberation of the bikes and stared as the three grew fuzzy and disappeared. Another shot, a bullet ripped across her shoulder, blood spurted momentarily before the battle suit resealed itself, cutting the flow. They also had weapons that could penetrate her body suit, it was supposed to be near armor proof and stop any human gunshots. This was getting very serious.

Crying in agony, she pressed her palm twice and vanished. Now neither could see the other, but that wouldn't last long as the colors were slowly beginning to shift in the alleyway. They had the means to descramble her invisibility cloak. *Yup, someone has access to my technology and that isn't someone from earth.*

It was hard to pinpoint where the others were in the rumble. The reek of rich exhaust filled the air. She stumbled over one of the three she'd already taken out and pulled his gun free. Her body beginning to shimmer into view, they were tuning into her frequency.

A shot rang out. Sherida twisted aside. Too slow, as a bullet ripped into her arm. She hit the ground and rolled squeezing off two shots in the direction of the shots. A cry, metal buckling, glass shattering, metal screaming in protest, assured her she'd hit one of them.

With less bikes running it was easier to pinpoint her targets. Sherida squeezed off another round, rolling, just as her arm came into view. They'd pegged her frequency. The metallic crash and screech of another motorcycle let her know she'd shot another one.

White tracers bearing death whizzed all around her as she dove under one of the downed bikes. Blood splattered her shoulder as agony ripped through her. One bike left rumbling, he gunned the throttle. Bullets flashed over chrome, missing their intended target. The rage of heavy hog under throttle bellowed up and down the alley.

Aiming about two feet off the ground she emptied the gun at the approaching biker. A fireball lit up the alley as all remnants of her invisibility cloak vanished. She stood up on wobbly legs, blood streamed onto the ground. Her circuits were attempting to stop the blood flow in order to begin repairs, the body suit resealed itself again, but the gunshots were in bad spots. She needed to go into cocoon and recuperate from the wounds. But first she needed information before the world discovered what had transpired here as the haze of concealment rippled away. She would not be able to dispose of the damage first.

The last biker blown off his hog lay in a crumpled mess. He still moved, the others were dead.

Sirens wailed. The authorities were quickly approaching. She staggered to the fallen biker and grabbed him by the collar. "Who set you up to this?"

The sirens were coming up the street. She could probe his mind, but she didn't have the luxury of time. "Tell me now or die," she growled.

Her hand constricted around his throat.

"If I tell you I'm a dead man."

"If you tell me I'll let you live, and leave it up to you to deal with whomever." His face began to turn blue as she crushed his windpipe.

"Okay," he gasped.

The screech of tires, sirens blaring and the thud of doors sounded at the end of the alley.

She eased up on his windpipe a little.

"Don't know his name," he croaked out. "We contact him through the box, he gave us the guns and descrambler." Sweat poured down his face, he sputtered through blood oozing from his lips. She spied the black cigarette shaped case nestled in his shirt pocket.

"Did you use this to break my cloak?"

"Y-yes."

"Police! Freeze!" Echoed from the far end of the alley.

Too late. The biker smiled, probably happy for the only time in his life to see police officers.

She hit her palm twice and vanished. Sherida twisted his neck violently until it snapped. There could be no survivors as she grabbed his case and staggered backwards. The thump of the police officers' boots and the background wail of other sirens echoed.

"What the..." one of the two closest sputtered as they reached the dead biker. "I could have sworn I saw someone in black hovering over this guy."

"Well, there's no one here now Melvin," the other replied. Melvin stared as he thought he saw a trail of blood drops appear leading away from the biker.

"Oh man, I've been working too long."

Roger stopped his lawnmower for a moment. A stray dandelion had the audacity to wreck the untouched green carpet of his lawn so he hit it with a shot from the pesticide that hung holstered to his side. "Take that." He returned to the lawnmower he'd been sweating over for the last hour.

He caught Mrs. Miller dusting her steps. After the other night, Roger decided to take a break and see her.

"Hi Mrs. Miller."

"Oh, hi Rog, I didn't hear you sneak up. Quite the storm we had a couple of nights ago." She smiled at him as she rested on her broom.

"Yes, it was. I had to retrieve my mangy mutt from your yard during that horrible weather."

"Your butt? What's wrong with your butt? Let me guess, you're suffering from those infernal hemorrhoids. My poor husband Charlie used to cry in agony some days, every time he went to the bathroom, you know."

"No. Not butt, Mrs. Miller. I said mutt," Roger spoke loudly.

"Pardon me, I don't think I've got my hearing aid on." She searched in her ear.

Roger thought a moment while she floundered to get her ear piece. "Oh, and thanks for giving Sparky that bone the other night. He sure enjoyed it."

"Phone? Oh, sure. Go use my phone if you like."

"No, bone!"

"Oh sorry. But I haven't given your dog any bones lately." She looked puzzled as she fitted the piece in firmer.

Roger was puzzled. "Well if you didn't, where did he get that large bone from?"

"Large bone you say? He must have got it from that kook I've got staying in the garage." She searched in her pockets for her other hearing aid.

"What kook?"

"Oh, some guy who I never see about. All I know is that he's got that garage locked up tight and I never see him. He's always got my nine hundred dollars rent money in the mail slot on the last day of the month mind. Said he was some sort of taxidermist."

"He pays you nine hundred for that old garage?"

"Yup." She motioned him closer. "I figured he'd got one of those grow-ops in there. Only I read in Reader's Digest that there'd be a funny smell and he'd have all the windows boarded up. I watch my electrical bill you know and it's the same as always. I never see him come and go, which suits me fine."

"Wow. Well I don't think he's doing anything illegal in there, other than extorting dinosaur bones for small dogs. Most curious," Roger muttered, as he began to walk back to his lawn cutting. "Thanks Mrs. Miller, somehow I had a hunch you'd say something like that."

"Lunch? Yes, I do believe it's time for lunch." She patted her pockets looking for her hearing aids as she walked into her house. "Now where are those infernal hearing aids again?"

"They're in your ears." He shook his head as he walked. *Crazy old gal. Only who'd pay that kind of money for a lousy garage. Obviously someone that wants privacy. Weird.*

Chapter Six

"*Many get lost on the duality of desire. Like everything else it bears a positive and a negative aspect. Balance for some is hard as the edge is thin.*"

I reached forward, hoping to ground myself against the coolness of the rock, wanting to release this damning throb building inside. Instead my hand encountered another hand. Soft, warm, it was the woman of the drawing and I was he or was she me? She smiled, sparkles of crystal dust flew from her eyelashes. She smiled again and joy sprang as she touched my chest. Naked, I was naked. As I looked over, I realized she was too. The electrifying heat of her hands caused moans to erupt from my throat. Another caress, but of want, not closeness.

I closed my eyes. I wanted her, but I wanted more than just base sex. What I really wanted was the deep connection I felt when making love with Beth.

Her lips drew against mine yet those lips felt so familiar and I opened my eyes and those of my Beth stared back at me. We kissed deep from the soul, like so many times I've done this before with Beth, her lips and my want pulled me from the waters and washed me away into the realm of lovers.

We were alone, incense filtered the air. Candles sprung from the darkness, the silk of the bed flowed under us. I held her. Moans as her breasts, fire-points of erotic energy, swayed back and forth. Gasps, moans rang out, more hers, then ours. I reached down, wetness flowed from her. A sweet river of desire. She gasped in her need and licked at my ears, my throat. Needing me, wanting me inside of her.

I fell backwards into the dew of a soft forest grass, wildflowers speared scents into the air, showering us. Aromas of delicate sensuality, chamomile, honeysuckle, patchouli and jasmine flooded the air. The woman's face changed to Beth as she slid on top of me, inserted me into her wetness. I shuddered, every inch of my hardness searing against the heat of her, while her skin, cool to my touch, sent shivers of electricity across me. Fire and ice, heat and water. Passions embracing each other, racing into desire's maddening headlong lust.

We made love again and again, until, totally spent, I lay in complete contentment. Where I could lay forever. She rose and I realized I was now in a cubicle in a room surrounded by curtains of silk. All around many other couples were moaning, making love. Lost in their passions, consumed by desire. What was going on here?

'Lost in passion's embrace.' Isn't that what the Hathor said? I rose limp, weak, she brought two glasses and offered one to me. It contained heady red wine. I wanted water, something to slake the thirst, not sap my will even further and stir what I didn't have left inside to stir, to pull me under.

I reached for the other glass. It contained a clear liquid, which I knew was water, sobering, revitalizing water. "Come, instead, to me, my love."

Beth lay on a bed of silk, rose petals spread all around. Smelling of earth and rain forest. Her legs opened slowly, inviting me into that open forest of passion and delight. "No, I can't."

I'd already stayed too long, anymore and I'd become slave to my own lust. I knew this, still I lingered. Other women slid past the veils of silk and entered the room. Tall voluptuous blondes, petite oriental ladies, luscious dark beauties.

"Let us give you pleasure, massage you. We will make you aroused again." They held bowls of oils, smelling of patchouli and ylang ylang.

"No, I can't."

Two began to kiss each other before me. Shedding their clothes, hands fondling breasts with nipples erect, stroking each other between their legs. "Then stay, watch us instead."

One of my strongest fantasies, most males. "I ... I ..." can't died on my lips.

Arousal began again. Two other women joined them and kneeled. They began to pleasure the ones standing with their tongues between the curls of softness between their legs. Moans of Sapphic desires. So hard to take my eyes away, women arousing each other.

Beth reached for the cup of water and offered me the wine. "Stay just a little longer. If you're tired perhaps one of them can entertain me."

Two women threw their heads back and moaned as they pulled closer the two on their knees. Moans of other lovers ghosted through the room, calling to me to join them or watch. I had to go, to stay and drink the wine would be too much. Lost in sybaritic pleasures.

"Yes, stay and let me do the same to you, as she does to me." The tall blonde pulled at the back of the head of the dark skinned girl licking at her. Sights of pink tongue darting through the dark triangle, shuddering as the throes of orgasm ran through her body.

"No, I can't." So hard to utter now. My desires returning at the sight, I wanted to join them as most men fantasize about.

I must go. I grabbed the glass of water, drank deeply and looked up. I was no longer in the room but back in my bed.

Roger sat in his usual booth at the diner across the street from his work with Bill Richards, his co-worker and best friend since childhood, they'd just returned from the washroom where Roger had shown him the fresh scar behind the Band-aid.

"Jeezus you don't screw around. You already had surgery? How in the hell did you get this to happen?"

"Let's just say I was so pissed after missing two flights that I paid for the damn surgery myself. No way was I gonna miss my honeymoon or be strip searched again. It didn't really hurt and seems to be healing very fast, other than the fact that I am still shitting petroleum jelly out."

Bill laughed, "tell me about it. Well this is even going to sound stranger. I had the same thing happen about two years ago on a business trip to the Orient."

"What? You're kidding me."

Bill was great at bullshitting and usually the life of the party, he unbuttoned his shirt. "See, in almost the same place as yours. Didn't show up on x-rays as metal, but it is. Only two years ago there weren't any bomb scares so customs had no problem letting me through. Figured it was a glitch in their machine and like you didn't want to take a chance it getting delayed or missing a flight."

Roger took a sip at his coffee while Bill tucked his shirt back in. "Do you have the fragment?"

"Yeah, I keep it in my vest pocket. Of course I don't have it on me. I did keep it though. Somewhere in the house."

"Tell you what, I'll bring mine over on the weekend. I wonder if they are the same material, similar shape as well."

"Sure, sounds good. I should be able to find it. Besides, Shirley wants to get that cabbage roll recipe from Beth. Make sure she brings it."

"Deal." They got up to leave. Roger plunked a couple of dollars down on the table for the tip.

"Hey, did you get any of that really good Hawaiian Maui wowie?" Bill asked as they walked out.

"Smuggle Mary Jane across the border, after the scar incident, that's as bad yelling Hi Jack at the airport. Like I'm going to toke up over there. Give me a break. Besides the two guys I asked were all out. Bad time of the year, I guess." Not that he'd ever try to buy any there or anywhere. He merely said it to humor Bill. Toking was one thing, buy drugs a whole other matter.

As Roger walked away it dawned on him. *Not a coincidence*, his guts were telling him.

Sherida leaned against the wall in the dark alley only three blocks away from where all hell had just busted out as the humans began to discover the bodies of the bikers. They'll probably regard it as another gangland killing in their eyes.

Already her internal circuits were sealing off the wounds, preventing further blood loss. If it wasn't for her cybernetics she'd be dead already. She couldn't go any further, losing too much blood. Reality began to spin away. She needed to get away, to a safe place, if there was any such place here, now. It appeared that the connection to home wasn't safe either.

"Rest," she gasped and slumped onto the ground. The stink of garbage, urine and moldy debris filtered in. She needed to heal first. Her body internals beginning to shut her down.

She held the black box tight as she pulled back the fake skin over her left arm. Myriad fingers of plasmic circuitry swarmed under the surface of her skin. Bio-engineered chips stared back at her. This was probably how they were tracking her.

Only a scant few on her home world knew about her mission, but this box was definitely Federation material and with no established protocol it meant only one thing. No one was to be trusted.

Sherida closed her eyes and screamed in pain pulling one of the organic chips from her arm. Blood poured from the wound, quickly stopping. She fell into the garbage as the world spun away in dizzying circles. The chip she used to contact the Council and, she knew from her training, the only way Council had of reaching her, possibly tracking her. Her eyes fluttered, she needed to move and get away. Yet her legs didn't have the strength to stand her up as she tried and collapsed into a heap.

Grabbing a broken liquor bottle she smashed the communication chip like a cockroach on the sidewalk and did the same to the black box. Now she was alone, cut off from her Home-world, Council, everything. Alone and blind, a billion light-years from home.

Her body was about to shut down in order to heal itself.

A mangy alley-cat sent a garbage can lid clanging to the concrete as she fell, pulling some old newspapers over her head, covering herself and the world went black.

Roger looked up from the flames of the gas fireplace. "Shirley, that was one fine meal." Shirley just nodded concentrating on her scrabble game with Beth. Both cutting edge competitive types.

"I tell you, get those two together and they'd play Scrabble until the tiles wore out."

Bill smiled as he held the irregular piece of metal in his hands. It gleamed, catching rays of light as he turned it around. "Sure is shiny. You'd think after all this time inside me it should be rusty or corroded or something."

"Thank goodness it isn't, or we'd both have metal poisoning. But you know something, this piece is nearly the same size and shape as the one from inside me. Hang on." Roger got up and walked to the front entrance where his coat hung.

"Are you on drugs? That would be impossible."

"As a matter of fact I am." Roger snickered, they'd had a quick toke outside just earlier. He dug around in his pockets and took the piece of metal over to Bill.

"Wow, are you ever right." Bill held one in each hand and turned them around.

"Hold it one second, pal." Roger yanked them from Bill's grip as something caught his eye.

"Hey, what the… I was looking at those."

The girls looked up and in unison said "If you boys can't play together quietly we'll put you to bed." They laughed.

"Can it will ya. Sorry, Bill." Roger apologized and held the two shapes up to the flames of the fireplace. "For a moment, I thought I saw something funny."

"Ah, that's just the weed, man."

"No, I'm serious." Roger held the two objects nearly side by side, comparing the sides, turning each one around. They did indeed seem to match each other.

Bill blinked, "it does look like they fit together."

Roger moved the two pieces closer together and felt a strong pull start. "I can't keep them apart," he said struggling, they clinked together. "Holy!" He dropped the two metal fragments in shock and stepped back.

"Did you see that?" Bill bent over and nearly banged into Roger's head.

"See it? I felt it. It was like they suddenly became magnetized."

"Too frigging weird." He reached under the couch and pulled one of the pieces out into the light. "Where's the other chunk?"

Roger squinted into the shadows. "Don't see it." He straightened up, glaring at Bill's hand. "Shit. It's in your hand."

"No, I've only got one pie…" Bill stared and dropped the metal.

They watched as it hit the ground and rolled over. Both reached for their drinks and took a long pull. Neither making a move. Both freaked out.

"You pick it up."

"No. You man."

Roger gave it a nudge with his foot before slowly bending over and picking up the now larger piece. He stared at it before turning it around and then tried to pull it apart. "Not only can I not pull them apart," he stared closer, "but I can't see where the two pieces were separate. It's like they've welded together."

"Too frigging weird." Bill simply stared while Roger sank into the softness of the couch, examining every surface of the metal. Running his nail over it, trying to find a joint.

"Here, take a look."

"I ain't touching it. I'm totally freaked out here. Those pieces virtually jumped into each other. It was like they were waiting all this time to unite or something," he muttered to himself. "Like they were meant to be together."

Roger shook his head. "Now you're the one who sounds crazy. We need to think of something here, like when this could have happened." *This wasn't coincidence, yet how was this possible?*

"Like a minute ago."

"No, like when these things were put in us."

Bill fell back into the cushions. "Too frigging weird. You mean like we were implanted?" He went white. "Aliens, I've seen the movies, Man. They wake up and devour you from the inside out."

"Gimme me a break, now you're being paranoid. If they were to do that, it would have happened a long time ago. How about we'll talk some more at lunch tomorrow. I don't think neither you nor I are in any state of mind right now." He set the metal on Bill's mantel.

"You ain't leaving that thing here. In the middle of the night it opens up and a million little very hungry alien bugs come out of it and eat me alive."

"It's perfectly harmless," Roger smiled, "although I'd swear the two pieces don't weigh any more than the single piece did."

"Yeah, I'm going to leave a hunk of some sort of alien metal that was inside you and me, and has suddenly merged into a bigger section on my coffee table, not leaving a mark behind. Are you nuts? I've seen Species, Aliens and Attack of the Bladder Beasts From Hell. That thing will come alive and devour me in my sleep. No way."

"You're being overly paranoid. Okay I'll take it with me, I think I'll give our resident alien spiritualist, Theodore a call tomorrow."

"Spiritualist? He's a whack job, sniffed one too many incense cones, he has." Bill blurted, obviously completely freaked by this point.

"Now you're being an ass." Roger put the piece into his pocket and walked over to Beth. "Time we were leaving."

"Why, won't Bill play with you anymore?" The girls snickered.

"Go ahead, the game's nearly over and I can't beat you." Shirley smiled.

"Let's go, please," Roger demanded as he headed for the front door, making sure the metal was still in his pocket. *Only Bill was right, it wasn't about releasing aliens this was about releasing something inside him or me. Is this what has been causing the weird dreams lately?* He could feel the vibrations coming from the joined pieces. *Like they were sending a signal or...* He closed his eyes and began to see visions of beings like the ones from his dreams. "Hey, have you been getting any strange dreams since this was cut out of you?"

Bill thought a moment, "yeah I did at first, but they ended pretty fast. Vaguely remember a temple complex and... and this weird tall being." He scratched his head. "I think he wanted to teach me something or take me someplace, I told him to beat it."

Roger screwed up his face. "Yeah, strange, me as well." He walked over to the girls.

"Well, I guess we're going." Beth leaned towards Shirley. "Wonder what the hell is stuck up his ass?"

Roger already had his coat on and was heading out the front door. He needed to head to bed. The visions were calling.

Bill simply sat and stared into the fire as Shirley hugged Beth goodbye. "Too frigging weird."

Memories of the last time that her mother's warm hand held hers flooded in. Her mother, Chakira, was taking her on a long walk in the sacred northern woods. They walked for several hours into the depths of the dense forest; somehow her mother knew the way, even though the trail was barely marked. They stopped in a clearing, before a small pond. She didn't know why they came out here, but she sensed that it was the time of the Telling in her life.

Hundreds of wild, multi-colored flowers littered the shores Butterflies fluttered among them and dozens rose as they sat down. For a moment the sun above was filtered with the iridescent colors cast from their wings. They rested against a large rock, allowing the heat to penetrate into their bodies. She knew these butterflies were sacred among her people, as was this pond.

Finally her mom spoke, breaking the sheer serenity and peace of the air. "As you know the time for your Telling, for you to discover what course your life shall take, is upon you. We are here where many of the villages' youth go to discover this. In your case it is before the child rearing years begin."

"But I don't want to go anywhere. I love it here with you and Father."

"Yes, it might or might not be so. We, as you know, trust the universe guides us down the correct path already chosen for us. Stay here." Her mother got up and looked for certain flowers to pick.

Returning, she crushed them into two small bowls she pulled from her pockets. "Now breathe down and we shall enter dreamtime together."

The overpowering pungent aromas flooded her nose. Her mother breathed deeply, her head fell back and she was asleep. Sherida began to breath deeply also as a sound broke the stillness. A feral low growl broke the air. She gagged, pushing away the aphrodisiac fumes wafting from the bowl. Her head spun, she staggered upright, trying to fight off the dizzying effects as a Leercat came into view. "Mother?"

But she didn't move, well under the influence of the scented flowers. Sherida also knew that if she awoke she wouldn't be allowed to interfere with what was unfolding. The cat wasn't nearly her size, but she knew from others in the village that they had a nasty tendency to be vicious if provoked. *Either I lead it away from Mother, or?* She looked about. A large branch caught her eye, and several rocks. The cat growled again as it approached her. She shook her mother again, no use. Her mother was completely out.

The young girl snapped the branch into a four-foot section and held it naturally in front of her like a sword. The cat slunk slowly towards her, unsure of the lack of panic its prey was portraying.

She saw it limped slightly; an eight-inch scar shone on its right front leg, oozing red and puss. An injured Leercat was even more dangerous. *It thinks we are easy prey.*

Sherida held her ground, twirling the branch before her. She knew if it sensed her fear it would have already attacked. *So, you are weaker than I think.* Its slavering jaws hungered for her flesh. Her voice told her. *I must be brave and take the attack to it.*

She grabbed two rocks, screamed in a loud, shrill voice and ran towards it. She flung one with deadly accuracy at the beast. The rock grazed off the injured quarter. The cat cried in agony and, not wanting any of the fight about to begin, it turned and blood oozing from it, it bolted into the safety of the forest. Emboldened, Sherida ran after it a few feet, screaming her rage and new-found bravery. She stopped, panting, as tears of panic erupted from her eyes. It was the bravest and craziest thing she had ever done.

I must be crazy, she thought as a hand touched her shoulder. Her mother smiled down at her. "The universe has decided. You will go tomorrow to begin your training for the ranks of our defenders. I shall always love you and will miss you."

It would be the last time she was with her mother alone. The Angelic Corps came to begin her training as a defender of their world the next day. She hadn't seen her family or home since then.

If I live through this I will be allowed home. Her head fell into the smelly refuse a million light years from where she was born.

Roger sat at the breakfast table, his head dizzy. A weird dream still haunting him, of being by a lake shore, laughing with some others, only who he couldn't remember when he was younger.

Beth had given him supreme hell last night for leaving so abruptly and rudely. He'd apologized, realizing he deserved it. He didn't tell her much about the metal fragments. Other than the fact the two seemed to weld together and Bill more so than himself were a bit freaked. Would she believe him? Hell, he didn't believe it himself truly. He'd called Theodore who seemed a lot more rational than Bill and set up a meeting at the end of the week before their usual poker night without the girls.

Lifting the morning paper he stared at the headlines. 'Wife of Potential Governor Candidate arrested and charged with the brutal slaughter of her two children, claims a crocodile did it.'

"This is wild." As Roger read the article he caught Sparky chewing on one of his bones out of the corner of his eye. He thought of the other night and of his angel spirit. Why would she be there, of all places? Unless there was something wrong or really bad in Mrs. Millers garage.

The only other times he'd remembered seeing his angel was when he was in danger, real danger. Roger was sixteen, he had just got his driver's license three months earlier and had picked up Jeff and Mike. They'd got a case of beer with Jeff's fake ID, due to the fact he'd whiskers early and looked much older. The three were heading over to a friend's for a party. Cocky, he has driving like an ass gunning the car and pretending to be a race car driver, showing off the car's capabilities to his buds.

"This car grabs the road with hunger. Watch me take this corner," his last words as the squeal of tires, protesting their attempt to grip the pavement, exploded in everyone's ears. The roar ripped from the headers of his 69 Camaro's 350 engine as he geared down into second. Driveline shuddered as he punched the throttle again. Sheer exhilaration, power, all three hundred horsepower, his to control under the touch of his foot. Heady things to a testosterone poisoned teenager.

Their laughs cut short by the horrible sound that destroyed his alcoholic madness. The snap of exploding u-joints and driveshaft hammering the body of his car. Someone yelling, "what the fuc- -"

The sharp blast of headers in deceleration. Driveshaft dug into pavement, spinning the car around. Bomb-like explosion of his front tire letting go, unable to take the load thrust on it. Glass exploding everywhere. Imbedding into his face, blinding him. No control. The sickening sensation of tumbling over and over. The snap of his leg bending beyond points it was meant to bend as everyone was thrown around, long before the days of mandatory seatbelts. Final searing unconsciousness as head smashed against steel door.

How much time he was out Roger never knew. Probably not long. Gagging on the noxious smell of burning rubber and the raw stench of gasoline. He was in a crumpled heap, upside down seat belt trapping him in. Roger screamed in agony as someone pulled at his leg. Blood blurred his vision.

Someone pulling at him? Through the black smoke haze, and alcohol's delirium his body being dragged and dumped on the grass a few feet away. Fading in and out of consciousness he stared into the face of a concerned angel. Eyes of the blackest black with lines sweeping away, looking vaguely Chinese, but her hair, a platinum snow white. It glowed in the pale of the night. Certain he was alive she turned and started towards the car. He remembered the slender figure of a woman running back to the car dressed in black.

Jeff's moaning bringing him back as he was also dumped beside Roger. She turned to get Mike, only a searing fireball of heat blasted him, engulfed his car, lifting it. Police sirens wailed from around the corner. Wordlessly, she pressed something on her arm and began to shimmer, vanishing into the night as the police cars screeched to a halt.

He never told the police about her, although the officers couldn't figure out how two guys, both with broken legs, could crawl from the wreckage.

"The last one not so lucky he didn't make it out," one of the officers spoke as the fire trucks arrived.

He'd never forget the angel with the sing-song voice, and her parting words, "I'm sorry. Protocol, I had to save you first." *So why was that so important?*

Mandolins twanged in longing serenades to lost loves as violins and harps vibrated melodic melodies by practiced fingers dancing over them.

Tom opened his eyes. The symphony flowed in harmony to synchronistic rhythms like a school of fish flowing one way then another, to the orchestrations of the conductor and the currents of the ocean.

"What the hell is going on here?" He looked around the concert hall, most of the audience had their eyes closed, no doubt, feeling as well as hearing the music rising in crescendos around and over them.

"I don't like opera, nor classical. Jazz is more my bag."

"Some need to tolerate what they don't understand," spoke a tall thin being, dressed in long flowing robes, sitting beside him.

Someone from the artsy-fartsy crowd, a director or crazy professor type, Tom mused.

Horns kicked in, delicious rich French horns. Trumpets and bass drums cascaded as cymbals crashed.

"I don't understand."

"I am an instructor."

"Of what, some crap-shit opera house?"

"No, of life."

"What life?"

"Why yours, of course."

"I don't need any more instructions. I'm doing alright in my career. Hang on, I've seen you before." Tom glanced around. "In fact, I've been here many times before. Yes, I've dreamt this before. You're here to teach me something. Woo-woo stuff. Energy zones or some such."

"Chakras."

"That's it, chakras. Does that have something to do with the East Indian stuff? You know Tantric things like the Kama Sutra, with all those hot sexual positions."

"That is more the realm of the second chakra. Which in your case will probably be your greatest challenge." The Hathor shook his head and rose from his seat.

"Challenge? Sex? You gotta be kidding me. I've never had a problem with that. Either getting it up, or talking to women and getting hooked up."

The Hathor stood emotionless. "Your survival skills are great. The ability to deduce, problem solve, is highly defined. But you lack seriously in the spiritual realm. That is why I'm here."

"To open my mind, make me become one with the universe and all that. Heck I thought I already did that whenever I get stoned."

"External stimulants don't open the chakras, if anything they shut them down, stunt them. This chakra, the first, is the root chakra. Its element is earth. It is of grounding, survival and stillness."

"That's cool stuff, guru boy. So what does survival, other than trying to stay awake, have to do with an opera?"

"Observe."

A thunderous explosion tore apart the stage. Wood and metal instruments shattered the air. Two other explosions thumped bodies into the air, shattering rows of content audience into pandemonium.

Tom dove to the floor. People screamed, stampeding towards the rear doors as smoke poured into the building and dust shuddered down from rafters.

He could hear people crushing themselves over others in the frantic melee. "No better than a stampeding herd of mad lemmings. So much for being spiritually enlightened." He coughed and looked around noticing that the holier-than-thou dude was gone. Another explosion ripped loose the balcony and sent it crashing down onto the dozens trying to fight their way out.

"No good, need to find another exit." Tom crawled along the floor trying to find air, which he knew was best along the ground. Moans and screams tore at his ears. Blood splatters everywhere. Through the haze a red glow from near the side of the stage.

"Fire exit." He blinked, coughing twice. Smoke was billowing in, black and acrid, from a spreading fire. He didn't have long before the entire structure went up taking all inside with it.

He scurried over abandoned concert guidebooks, leather shoes, jewelry and even the odd wig. Agonizing moments later he gripped the door's lever and pushed. "It's jammed." Tom rammed the door with all of his might. Sunlight cracked the smoldering haze.

"Help me," a voice cried.

He looked behind him and saw an elegantly dressed young woman. Her face smeared with makeup and blood. Next to her a young boy, his face limp. Tom stared closer, the face; so like himself at that age.

Another thump shook the building. "It's going to collapse any second." He reached for the pretty young woman and stopped. "I've done this before."

Terrible groaning, bricks splintering under tremendous strain. Tom grabbed the young lad and heaved the two of them through the gaping fire exit.

"Well done. You are learning."

Tom smiled and dropped the boy to the ground outside as sirens sounded and blackness billowed from the door. "Chakra, schmackra.

I'm going back in to save the babe." He disappeared into the smoking rubble.

The Hathor closed his eyes. "Learning for some is a painful journey, done again and ..."

The entire building imploded. Tom woke with a start.

"...again."

Roger sipped at his coffee, still waiting for Bill, who had yet to show up for lunch. He'd texted, "running late." But not to leave without seeing him as he had something important to talk about.

Just as Roger's meal arrived Bill come storming into the restaurant. "Hey Rog, I got it."

"Got what? I thought you'd stood me up on purpose. Man did Beth ream me out over our catatonia of the other night?"

"That's what I want to talk to you about. The night those hunks of metal were put into us. I think I got when."

"What do you mean the night they were put into us?"

"When it happened. It just dawned on me. Remember when we went to that summer camp about twelve years ago? I think there were six of us. We'd snuck a case of beer from the counsellors' office and canoed over to the island in the middle of the lake."

"I don't remember anything about beer and a canoe..." Roger hesitated. Trying to recall the night in question. "I only remember all of us waking up the next morning with splitting headaches."

"That's the night, and that was all I could remember at first too. Now think hard. What led up to us waking with a hangover? I think the memory was wiped from us and maybe because I didn't tune into the weird dreams like you have that instead the memory was released in my mind."

Roger looked like at him like he was on some strange drugs but before he blurted out something stupid Roger looked up and the words played themselves over in his mind. "Well let's see. I recall there was you, me, Theodore, Andy, Fred and Mike Amberside. Yes, six. We were all staying in the back cabin."

"Right."

A haze began to lift, like opening an old forgotten book for the first time in many years. "Yes, we'd snuck down to the girls' cabin wanting to wake some up, only they were all already asleep. So Mike had the bright idea of going over to the counsellor's cabin and came back all excited because he'd spotted two cases of beer sitting on the back porch. I remember now, the electricity had cut out for a while and we figured they put the beer outside to cool down."

"We went down to the beach to crack them open." Bill bulged his eyes at Roger.

"No," Roger gasped a moment, memories unfolding. "Yes. Only we didn't have any church keys so we broke the ends off on the rocks. I remember now, I was afraid of getting glass stuck in my throat." How had I forgotten that? Was he right? Had it been purposely forgotten.

"Yeah and Theodore snuck off to get a couple of glasses and an old shirt to use as a filter." It was coming back. Why had he forgotten all that? His recollection was usually good.

"Hell, I think we spilled more beer then we drank."

"So do you remember what happened next?"

"No, I remember waking up with a massive headache and ..." Roger stopped. As they talked more things began to sort themselves out and surface through the murk. "I remember Theodore not drinking anything, he was kinda religious or something. And I remember sitting out on the dock. Stars brilliant overhead and lights, lots of lights."

"Right, that's where my memory stopped until last night. I remember lights too and Theodore sitting off on the beach watching us. I remember the lights, only they weren't coming from the sky but from the water. And that's about all that comes to me."

"Lights in the water?" Roger thought hard. Buried memories lurching back through the haze of time. "I remember us running around on that pier. I remember the sky filled with lights. I vaguely remember us getting in major trouble and not talking about it after that. I thought we were just really drunk."

"On two beers? Get real."

"Yeah, that was the embarrassing part. Only thing that explained the hangover like headache." Roger peered at Bill. "So what makes you think it was there?"

Bill stared back. "I had a medical exam a week before that trip for an upcoming field trip to Europe. Most of the others in the group probably did too, they took x-rays and we had a major exam. So I doubt the metal was put into me before then." Bill stared at him again, "You don't remember the lights in the water then, do you? Think hard."

Roger closed his eyes and pulled himself back again to that moment in time. It was nearly twenty years ago. Running around on the dock, laughing, feeling blasted. Laughing and laughing. The guys all goofing around and… Theodore yelling.

From underneath. In the water something moved upwards. Roger opened his eyes. "The water, it began to get lighter, like Christmas lights blinking. How did I forget that?"

He opened his eyes, "Yes my God. I remember now, it's coming back to me. Theodore running off the dock, he wasn't playing on the beach. He was scared, 'Lights, lights in the water,' he said yelling at us."

"We all laughed thinking he was jerking around with our heads."

"Only we all turned when a glow began from below the surface. I remember we walked to the pier all cocky and stared into the water where he'd been standing on the edge of the pier." Flashes of memories fluttered by, wisps of recollections, dust disturbed. Roger thought. Why had he forgotten all of this? Why couldn't he remember anything else other than the lights? The dancing lights in the dark water. A long silence as they both sipped at their coffee.

"Yes." Bill said "and that's all I remember."

"But you remembered how?"

"Last year I went for a physical and the doctor noticed this growth." He pointed to the spot where a faint scar showed. The same area as Roger had his. "I didn't tell anyone except my wife, in case it was cancer. Like you a simple operation and lo and behold a hunk of metal. The doctor had no explanation, I kept it in my drawer and forgot about it, until I started to get odd dreams. That's when I remembered about the lights. It slowly came back to me and probably will to you at some point."

"Yeah, I did have a strange dream about being by a lake just the other night. Maybe getting the stones out does that begin to trigger some inner subconscious memory?" A long pause ensued, finally Roger spoke. "So the question is what did really happen after that and what did this to us? And Why?"

"I want to know more importantly, who they are." Bill stared at Roger, fear haranguing a wild streak in the dance of silence between them. "I think we need to get the group together and talk to Theodore. He knows all about these weird kind of cosmic woo-woo stuff."

Chapter Seven

*J*ungle abounds everywhere, filling me with humidity and freshness. This could be South America, only when I look up, two moons glow overhead. Something glistening with a gold tint catches my attention. A building, in the distance, a temple topped in gold.

After about an hour of walking the jungle parts and before me is a courtyard with four glistening pyramids. There, sitting before them, is a bizarre creature carved of stone. I stare up between the two paws up at the leonine face that is a replica of the Sphinx at Giza.

In a few scant steps we were inside the Sphinx and walking down a dark corridor with hundreds of paintings.

I wanted to ask if this place was like a school when the being said, "This place has been called many things, but a school would be the term most appropriate for you."

Before it could respond my thoughts betrayed me. "A school for what?"

"The mysteries."

"The mysteries of what?"

"The mysteries that are unfolding."

There was so much I wanted to ask, yet this wasn't the time. Now was the time to begin and do.

"I don't understand. You are so vague."

"Confusion is a good state to be in, like chaos."

"All you're giving me is riddles and psycho-babble."

"I can only say this. When you go through any transformation there is always chaos, disorganization. As one thing transmutes to another the fear of the unknown comes alive, awakens. Why do you think people become trapped in unhappy lives?"

"Don't know. They can't like it, yet they stay."

"The fear of the unknown, the chaos of not knowing, stops them advancing from the lesson before them. They do not have the necessary ingredient to want to continue their development as beings of this universe."

"And what is the necessary ingredient? Is it to learn and advance?"

"This is for you to discover, as you begin the journey. Enter the picture when you are ready."

"Enter? It's only a picture." I turned and the being was gone. I was alone in the vast hallway. Hundreds of pictures lined the walls, each depicting some sort of happening or scenario. I walked slowly until one picture in particular caught my eye, a woman crying at her kitchen table. Dishes were piled in disarray behind her; before her on the table sat a bottle of liquor, nearly empty, another was strewn on the floor. She looked and reminded me of my mother. I lurched as the stale must of old beer flooded my senses. Her despair, the haunted forlorn look. Such sadness seeped out at me. An intimate loneliness eked through her at me. I knew her childhood, her entire life was one of misery and being unloved. Only someone to clean, cook and get laid.

Pigments danced before me. Painted in such a fashion, they drew me in, Mesmerizing, drawing me.

She, my mom, was so utterly miserable in the marriage to my dad. That was clear to me now. Why did she stay? Was it to raise us kids, me?

I reached forward. How could the artist do that? With what medium … oils? I swore the paint was still fresh and wet.

Touching her eyes I stared at the bottle before me. Stale alcohol wafted upwards in stenches of grapes and rye, fruits and grains of the life-giving earth, perverted into pleasures to numb the mind and corrupt the pureness of the soul, steal at my will.

My guts burned, not enough food inside. My head throbbed as if I was hung-over. Was hungover? I suppressed the brief urge to puke, only because there was nothing inside me to release. Light from the outside world hurt my eyes. Eyes so heavy and swollen. Water, I needed water.

Is that what this picture did? Made you feel everything the subject felt? Or merely to draw you into his visions?

I rose, my body moving yet it was not me that seemed to move. As if I was in a dream state or one of ...

Lighter, I felt lighter. I turned around and instead of the hallway saw the rest of the kitchen. I clutched at the countertop, heard the click of nails on Formica and stared at my hands.

Fingernails, on long slender fingers. Varnish chipped, manicure overdue. Delicate fingers.

No, this couldn't be. I closed my eyes and pinched myself. I opened my eyes and stared into the same delicate hands. I stared down at myself, saw my small breasts, the flare of my hips, the torn skirt. Again I closed my eyes, yet no matter how hard I shook my head and how many times I opened them, it was the same.

"No, this can't be happening." A woman's voice spoke, my voice.

"Oh, but it is baby." The sound of a male voice behind me. I turn and stare at my husband of the past seven years dressed in tee shirt, his beer sodden belly hung loose. He towered inches taller than myself.

Memories of drunkenness, of drugs, of mixed-up days and nights. And worse things. I stare into his eyes and see his hunger, his need for release, glinting in the darkness of his soul. The damning passion for dominance, for gratification from pleasures of the flesh as he wanted it and could have whenever he needed.

"I found the stuff." He smiled in a lustful sneer.

I stare at the jar of petroleum jelly. Saw the twist from the bulge in his pants and knew that the horror was only going to get deeper.

"I – I can't, I've changed my mind." Pleading, surely I could make him change his mind.

"Too late, besides you like it with lube, you know that baby."

"No, I don't, I don't want this, not this way."

He grabbed my arm and pulled me forward, his breath rank with beer.

"I should teach you a lesson and not use any lube, but because I love you I will this time."

This time. It had happened before and perhaps with compassion and connection between us it could be enjoyable, but not like this. This was degradation of my soul, marital rape. I couldn't break from his grip.

I was so weak. Is this how most woman felt? Overpowered in the face of male aggression?

He flips me around and slams me against the table. Bottles rattle a grizzly tune. "Come on baby, you love it from behind."

Love, this wasn't love, I thought as his hands pulled my skirt aside and yanked my panties down. Love had nothing to do with the slather of jelly along my rear. His one hand holds me against the table while he fumbles for his zipper with the other.

I want to throw up, the alcohol in my system turning sour inside. I feel I'm going to be sick. Am sick. This shouldn't be happening, but it is.

Searing pain fills me from behind. I feel him inside me, deeper, until I feel his coarse hairs rubbing on my rear. His hardness penetrating my soul. Perhaps another time this would have been pleasurable, but not like this.

My wifely duty, to satisfy my man, my mother always told me. Some perverse part of me had always accepted this. Close off my heart from the pain, and it will all be over soon.

The lube helped.

"Oh God, you're tight. Just how I like it and I know you do too." He laughed, his sour breath washes over me, gagging me. He leans closer, he reeks of booze and tobacco as his fingers pinch my nipples hard. I am trapped beneath his bulk.

Pain splashes all around. My head hurts, he doesn't care, doesn't love me. I want this to be enjoyable, like I know it can be, not like this.

"Stop, please, it hurts."

"Only at first. You enjoy it rough. Don't deny it."

"No, stop."

"I said, shut up and enjoy it."

He slams my head into the table. I feel myself going limp, wetness oozes from my mouth. Blood?

He thrusts again and again, I am a mere rag doll bouncing back and forth under his savage thrusts. "Oh yes, here it comes, just for you baby." He grabs my hair and pulls my head back. I scream in agony as he thrusts deep and heat explodes inside me. "Oh yeah, you get better each time."

The cry of a youngster. My daughter, woken by the commotion is coming down the stairs. "Mommy, are you okay?"

No, she mustn't see this. I can't have her know the degradation I will allow myself to be subjected to.

"Damn," he laughed as I feel his bulk rising from me. Only the stabbing pain remains as he pulls out and zips up his pants. "That was great. Hope you got off too."

Not caring, nor wanting to, he'd had his pleasure. No, not loving. Why do I do this to myself? My knees weaken and I fell them buckling. Bottles rattle as I slump over and fall into a chair. A drink, more than anything I need a drink right now to numb myself. My guts burn.

"You know, she'll be ready soon." He smirks as he digs in the fridge, pulls out a can of beer and pops it open with a hiss.

"For what?" My guts heave and I turn, and spew what I have into the kitchen sink. Horrors of my childhood scream past, I had been taken many times by my father. One of the reasons I left home so early. Now here I was, again.

He lets out a large belch.

"For me to teach her how to enjoy it like her mother." Calmly he turns and saunters out of the room. "I wonder what's on the sport channel. I think the Falcon's are playing."

I slip to the floor, jelly, sperm and blood oozing from me as tears splatter the linoleum.

"Are you okay, Mommy?"

I pull myself upright, and straighten my clothes as much as possible. Numbness threatens to take over, to erase the sensations welling inside, like so many other times.

Angela. I'd been named after angels. Only I'm not one and there aren't any around to help me now. Bile burns in my throat, sickness threatens to erupt again. How long? How many years will I allow this? And soon to my eight-year old daughter. The stark guilt slams into me.

I love my child more than anything, more than I love myself.

That's the problem, isn't it? I don't love myself enough to want this to stop.

"Mom, you okay?" My daughter walks into the room, puts her arms around me and simply holds me.

"Ah, just feeling sick, a flu or something." I lie.

"Oh, I love you Mom, everything will be okay, won't it? You can't get sick." My child, no matter what, loves me. Even though I can't.

"Hold me, just hold me, hon."

As she holds me I feel the love, the unconditional love, wash over me.

"Say it again, I need to hear it again." She began to cry.

"I love you Mom. Everything will be okay." I feel the deep love tearing inside, feel it wash away the pain and guilt. Words I'd never had the courage to utter before surge forth. "I love me too." Tears splatter over my daughter's hair as I cry uncontrollably. "And you. Mommy loves you too."

Not everything would be okay, but I have hope. There was a phone number a social worker had given me last month, which I'd just tucked into a drawer. It was for a home, a home for battered women who had no place to go.

"Come on, help me to the bedroom. I have to make a phone call. I can't do this any longer and I will not let this happen to you." I grit my teeth in determination for the first time in many years.

I blink and stare up at the face of the lady in the picture. I glance at the Hathor as it shimmers into view beside me, then down at myself and back at the picture. There is something odd about the lady I didn't realize. I hadn't seen the glint in her eyes before.

"So, what did you learn?"

I turn towards the tall being. "That in all of that despair and abuse, this woman managed to find hope. Tell me, was that an exercise or was that real?"

"What is reality but the ultimate illusion?"

"Sherida keeps saying that. I don't get it."

"Then you still have much to learn."

Chapter Eight

Sherida opened her eyes. She was alone in a large cellar. She remembered her instructor telling her group in the first minutes of her training, 'expect the unexpected' was the golden first rule. Immediately two explosions ripped through the walls of her classroom and her instructor grenaded into a fireball of flames. Three of the trainees burst into tears and collapsed into helpless bundles. Some stood shocked, and a couple beside Sherida surveyed the surroundings and dove into action, either propping desks up or grabbing whatever they could to defend themselves. Sherida and the two others progressed to the next level as the virtual images faded away and her instructor stood there grinning. The others were sent home.

'Always be aware and wary' became the byline of the three. Memories of those days flooded in as claggy earth called to her from the dark as she began her first training mission on her own. Above wooden boards creaked as if something prowled. The souls of the former trees shrieked their demise above her head. She closed her eyes, trying to focus. Distractions.

Thousands of grubs, worms, Millipedes, no longer living in the displaced earth, removed to form this cellar cried from the pits of their souls. An overwhelming cacophony of anger, death and HOW DARE YOU? Flooded her senses.

Three words, humanistic.

A plod of a footstep, behind her.

Another, closer.

A cuff upside the head before she could react.

HOW DARE YOU?

Again, hammered at her senses.

It was spiritual, not alive. Thorough the intense natural voices of the once living entities in this dark dank place, she got it. Not her objective.

Something just outside the perimeter of this place and the earthen walls; something stalked her.

Only this wasn't human. This was the creature I was here for.

She willed herself away from the enticement of the trapped spirit. That wasn't her mission here, just a delusional distraction meant to make her fail.

She stood on the warm alive earth just outside the lone hut. She scanned the bushes with her cyber implants. A shadow moved thorough the brush. It was night anyways, but she picked up the large feline stalking her. She closed down some of her sensory array as the noises of birds, grubs began to overwhelm again. The heat sync of the creature wavered and vanished. What?

Sherida glared around. It had the ability to alter its perception field. Hence a very dangerous predator, one rarely seen or taken on this planet. Far more deadly than the Leercat from her home world.

From her left something lunged at her. Sherida spun away, blood spurting along her side and it was gone.

Damn, she rolled into a crouch, adjusted her perception filters. It stalked around her like a Velusian Boxer, waiting to lunge in again after the mandatory eight count or just testing the mettle of its opponent.

She leaped forward somersaulting and swung an open fisted blow at it. A sneer from the black furred cat as she caught it off guard. Slitted yellow eyes opened in an insidious glare as she caught it just below the throat.

Rage hissed in a half gurgle, startled at being touched. More used to being the one doing the attacking.

Sherida spun around again aiming a kick to its head. Empty air answered.

It had moved in a heartbeat.

Claws raced along her other side. The first slash had already begun to heal itself. Only her abilities could heal so many wounds; did it know these cuts would slow down her attacking abilities?

The creature sneered as the smell of hot blood filled the air and it continued to pace around her.

Yes, it knew. I wasn't the first one here to do this.

No wonder it was so dangerous and the last test before graduating from the ranks.

Still many failed, many died. She only had to touch the small disc in her left palm to return her back to the craft orbiting the outer shell of this world. Only that meant failure.

She lashed at it with her laser embedded in her right palm.

It blinked and was beside her. Sherida spun away catching it in the gut. Claws lanced out and slashed away at the laser. Sparks flew and she tried firing again. The creature gleamed evilly at her as mere sizzles answered her request.

It also learns very fast.

The beast retreated and began to slowly regain its composure, breathing deeply.

Good, gives me time to heal. Already the wounds on the left side had stopped bleeding and had scabbed over. The right side had nearly done the same.

Just as she thought that, the black-furred creature leaped at her. Sherida jumped aside. Long rakish claws tore down her left side again. Reopening her wounds.

It's playing with me, teasing me and it can read my thoughts. Evil bastard.

The creature growled in return. Hungry for more it ran towards her.

"Play with this." She opened her right palm and a blast of white light hit it full in the eyes. Sherida hammered the blinded cat over the skull and tore off into the woods.

She needed time to think how to defeat this feline. Her objective wasn't to overcome the creature, but to retrieve a crystal from a monument located a few kilometers from her touchdown point. Still, she had been warned there would be opposition to overcome. Now she knew how many never made it past this last phase of training. One wrong move would probably cost her life.

After minutes of running her radar told her it was just ahead. Gaining quickly, she knew the cat was approaching from behind. If needed she would kill the carnivore, but she would rather not. She sensed the cat wouldn't have the same compulsions. What was worse than a killer, was one that toyed with its prey. She ran through her memory banks on the known inhabitants of this world. Only one entry said anything about the rare Panthess. A black feline that mercilessly hunted down all it fed on. One man's journal entry told about being chased for days, losing blood and skin with each attack, until he had nothing left. Even then his final journal entry was that it sat there watching him, with one functioning arm and both legs crippled as he wrote his last words into his journal. The journal survived, judging by the reports of the meager bits of flesh they found, his remains never to be found after he became dinner.

Sherida gritted her teeth as she ran. Even with her augmented muscles the feline was circling in front of her. Almost too late she sensed it ejecting from the dense brush; a swipe along her arm and her implanted return switch tore away. Blood streamed down her arm. He was making sure I didn't escape. I had about three hours until the ship would move to pick me up. This hunt was to the end.

It ripped another strip down her back and savagely licked at the moist blood, tasting her. Then spun away. Sherida collapsed, trying to quickly repair herself, but the damage was intense. She struggled to get to one knee. Everything spinning.

It ran in for the kill and instead swatted her aside. It's toying with me. She tried to focus and pretended to collapse. Blood everywhere, the beast unable to control its hunger dove to her. The smell driving it on.

She swung around and slammed into its groin, the beast howled in agony and fell to the ground. You should have killed me when you had the chance. One of the things she learned in training; don't hold back it may cost you your life in return.

Sherida got up and ran to the base of a large fern that looked like an overgrown fungus. All around the tree lay birds and rodents flopping like they were drunk. She collapsed and slowly began to climb up out of the cat's reach. Her vision began to blur. The smell intoxicating. She shut down all of her olfactory glands.

The creature slunk into the glade. It walked with a slow limp, obviously in pain and growled in her direction, but didn't approach.

Safe for now she closed her eyes and let her equipment take over.

"Okay make it three Buds, and two Coors Light for the skinny guys on a diet," Roger laughed. He and Bill had managed to contact Fred, Sam and Theodore. They had met in the old Seattle Pizza restaurant down the street from their former high school. Many an afternoon they had spent there instead of being in school, and many a night after the bars closed. One of the few licensed restaurants in those days that stayed open two hours later after the bars closed to get the ongoing party animals. They'd learned to order several beers after hours and would sit there drinking and partying.

"Hey, can it," Sam laughing with the others, trying to hide the fact he was mildly offended. He brushed back his comb-over hairdo to cover his prematurely receding hairline and patted his large belly. "It's all bought and paid for, boys."

"And what's your excuse Fred," Bill remarked, taking a long pull from his drink.

For a Saturday afternoon the pizza place was unusually empty, which suited the guys just fine. They'd been bantering about old times, past girlfriends, sports and hot cars. The only one who didn't seem too thrilled to be part of the reminiscing group was Theodore. He sat quietly, sipping at his non-alcoholic beer.

"What excuse?" Fred smirked, patting the largest beer induced growth protruding from the midsections of the guys. "That's not fat, it's backed up sperm."

"Still single, then?" Roger commented.

The others howled.

They'd hung out often occasionally getting together for poker games. Although Theodore rarely joined them, even when called, and the one Roger had the hardest time, having to really express the urgency of getting to this meeting. He only agreed after Roger told him about remembering the lights and the metal found in Bill and himself.

"Look guys, I hate to cut it short, but I gotta get going pretty soon," he spoke quietly and smiled. Roger remembered Theodore always being an easy-going lad, full of laughs. The smile seemed an unusual stranger on his face, he hadn't noticed the deep sadness inside. Whoever this morose stranger, bearing the body of his friend was, he wasn't sure.

"Hey relax and grab another brewski, will ya," Bill piped up.

"Look, I really gotta go," Theodore said as he got up. Roger smelt the bullshit excuse a mile away.

Bill glanced at him, "Ask him now before he leaves."

"See ya guys." Theodore flung some money on the table as he turned his back.

"Hang on a second, Theo. I called everyone here because I've some questions to ask about the summer camp all of us attended in seventy six."

Theodore stopped his face turning pale as if he knew where this was heading. "What about that camp?"

The others put down their beers and watched knowing something was going down. Roger glanced around at the suddenly taut faces. "How about the night we snuck the case of beer down to the dock and got drunk? Does anyone remember that night?"

"Camp? Beer?" They all looked blankly at him as if he'd suddenly announced he was gay, before the lights came on in their brains, like conveniently forgotten, or erased memory. After all this time Roger realized they'd never talked about it as he watched the switches being turned on.

"Yeah, what a night. I'd completely forgotten," Sam sputtered, the rest nodded in agreement.

Fred choked as he downed the last of his beer quietly.

"Remember?" Theodore said, his voice rising. He took a step closer and pointed a finger at Roger, eyes on fire. "I've been fucking remembering that night for the past couple of decades. I'd wake up in a sweat nearly every night for the first few years."

"You saw them then didn't you? The lights?" Roger egged Theodore on. He'd stumbled onto something here and wasn't about to let go.

"Remember? I don't need to 'remember'. Those lights still haunt me. Dancing. Filling the sky, the waters below us. Dancing all around us. In us. No, I fucking 'remembered' enough." Theodore turned.

"In us?" Roger asked, puzzled. He didn't remember that happening. "Where in us?" Although he already knew the answer.

"Dancing lights? All I remember is the pounding head as we woke up on the beach. Either those counselors had spiked that beer or it had gone skunky or something," Fred said.

"Can it, Fred, I don't need to be humored right about now," Roger spat. "I think we're on to something here."

"I don't remember anything except waking up on the bloody beach, sicker than a dog." Bill said.

Sam looked at Fred. "Yeah, neither do I?"

Theodore took a step away from the group.

"Walking away from your fears won't help you. Where inside of us, Theodore?" Roger was prepared to tackle him if he had to, right here in the restaurant.

"Walking away? I've done more searching for answers, out there and in here, than I care to say. I'm tired of running. You want to know where?" Theodore tore at his buttons, shaking. At least one of them had remembered that night, until Bill told him, he'd also forgotten it. But he knew Theodore hadn't forgotten anything, he'd remembered it all. Theodore yanked his shirt aside. There, where Roger feared, lay a red welt. The remains of an operation several years ago. Three inches of damning coincidence?

"Unbelievable!" Bill gasped.

"The nightmares finally stopped after the operation. Only I knew it wasn't over. Somewhere inside here I knew they'd be back to visit me again and tell me more stuff. Or worse, operate all over again." Theodore said quietly, a tear forming in his eye. "You're the lucky ones. Read 'Whitley Strieber's Abduction,' if you want to know what I know. None of you understand what I've done to rid myself of the memory of that night. Things I've studied and read, realizing we have no idea of what is really out there and what they want from us. And you know what really pisses me off. None of you remember, do you?"

They all nodded back.

"Fuck me."

Roger saw the gleam haunt his eyes. He was worried that Theodore was going to lose it, something about him suggested that the man wasn't all there, or even partly there, or maybe he'd awoken an old forgotten deep fear. He needed to wrap this up quickly before it got uglier.

"And it's better if you don't know." He re-buttoned his shirt and spun around, heading for the door.

"Theodore, stay," Roger hollered.

"No. I've spent too many years dreaming, being haunted, every time I see lights flashing I'm reminded. I just want to be rid of it. Goodbye."

Roger stood up and lifted his shirt. "Theodore before you go, take a look at this."

Theodore slowly turned and staggered backwards a step glaring at Roger's fresh three-inch incision like he'd seen an obscenely hideous leech attached to it. Time hung in suspension, each heartbeat paced with catatonia's numbing voice.

"Bill, show him yours."

Bill rose and opened his shirt Theodore's legs buckled. "No, I've seen this a million times before in my dreams, it can't be happening again," he gasped.

The room swam away into a merciful black void.

Roger rushed to grab Theodore as he slumped to the floor. "I think it's time to get out of here guys."

"What the hell is going on here," Fred and Sam said in unison.

"And why do I get an idea we ain't playing poker tonight?"

"I think Trudy is still out with the girls, my place is the closest, let's head there." Bill directed.

"I'll help Roger get Theodore into the car, will you guys grab the bill?"

Sam stared at Fred. "Will someone tell me just what the fuck is going on here and how come I get stuck with the bill?"

"My thoughts exactly," Fred added.

Roger and Bill pulled Theodore upright and began to march him to the door. "We'll tell you at Bill's place, let's go."

Bill looked at Roger as they dragged him outside. "So if Theodore had a chunk in him also, that meant the other two probably did too."

Roger nodded back.

"Great. This is going to be an interesting evening and yup, doubt we'll be playing cards."

Sam looked at Fred, "you know what the hell just happened in there and is going on?"

"Nope, but I think this is going to be more fun than watching the ball game or playing cards."

"Yup, you better have lots of beer and taco chips, could be an all-nighter."

Roger jumped behind the wheel, "I'll get a couple of cases on the way over if that's what it takes to humor the peanut gallery."

Sherida closed her eyes. Blood covered her body and dripped down the main stem of the tree. Below the Panthess slowly circled.

She didn't know why he hadn't torn her out of the branches and finished her off. Was it simply toying with me, teasing me some more with torture? Or was there another reason?

Sheer volumes of pain tore at her mind. Okay, beta blockers kick in. She felt her agony begin to subside.

Now, she scanned her memory banks. The new implanted technology within her began to take over and repair her vitals.

Or are you simply waiting until I heal and wanting to toy and torture me some more?

Her olfactory glands were being shut down automatically. Why?

'Highly hallucinogenic substance in the immediate atmosphere' fed back in her brain in response to her question.

My bio-mechanisms were protecting me, shutting down my nostrils, as well as heal me. Okay then, what is this tree and the hallucinogenic substance? 'Genus undiagnosed, but similar to a Polyphyletic Fungus. The vapors given off perform aphrodisiac and hallucinogenic qualities, similar in composition to Psilocybin, baeocystin, psilocin and also contains trace elements of Lysergic acid diethylamide only direct inhalation is 300% percent stronger than the mere smelling or taking of the drug'. Okay, explains why the Panthess is still circling me. I'm sitting in what is commonly called a giant magic mushroom tree that is laced with LSD. That is why it hesitates to attack and most likely will wait until I climb out of this overgrown fungus. Once the creatures mark or begin tracking their prey they use their olfactory senses nearly exclusively. That combined with the ability to read an opponent's thoughts, make them nearly impossible to capture or kill. Okay, shut down my olfactory senses completely and flush any signs of residue hallucinogens from my system. 'System healed 58% major muscle groups 90%. Basic functions 80%. Flushing of hallucinogens will take three minutes longer.'

Sherida could feel the buzz beginning to leave her mind. I can't completely hide my thoughts, unless. Can I get a subconscious filter activated?

'Searching data base, filters active, but for limited time of fifty-eight seconds.' Just enough time to rig something up for my furry friend. She tore her shirt from her body and grabbed several of the softer branches, crushing them until the juices soaked into her shirt.

The cat growled loudly and began increasing its pace, obviously sensing or knowing she was up something. It can't read my mind, but it knows my body is repairing itself.

Sherida closed her eyes and let her mind go blank. 'Filters are beginning to erode, including olfactory blockers.'

He ain't going to wait for me to heal completely and the beta blockers will kick out soon as well. If I don't make my move now he'll know what I'm up to.

Sherida wrapped up the squishy mess, already her olfactory senses were beginning to fail. Her outer senses were being overcome. It's bright outside. So before I begin to talk to little animals on tree stumps.

Sherida leapt from the tree and screamed out, "The only mistake you made is not killing me. So. I'm coming for you."

She ran straight for the beast. One hand behind her back, catching the normally aggressive cat off balance. It was expecting her to flee.

Puzzled the creature paused, unsure of what to do.

"Okay party time, furball." She took one stride closer and flung the wet mass directly into its face. It opened its jaws in rage as heavens exploded and gasping voluminous odors cascaded down its throat and nose. Eyes stinging in acidic agony, it swatted the shirt away and stared at all manner of beasts and winged serpents descending towards it. The beast swatted at empty air, full rage at being cornered by all manner of demons attacking it.

"Unlike you, I go for the throat first. I don't aim to toy with you, nor allow you to be tortured more than needed. I only want to live." Already the sky began to shimmer in iridescent colors. Crap, I'm getting stoned as well.

She spun around, the beast only saw a whirling dervish descending in a twirl as her leg crushed his midsection. A fist hammered down, a crack echoed away in the spinning corridors of its brain as Sherida splintered its jaw. One long fang broke away spinning in the air.

All the cat saw was termites screaming, as they swarmed by the millions towards it. Their jaws clacking in hunger, it tried scratching away in terror. Sherida lunged forward catching the fang and in one deft move she drove it deep into the feline's heart. Blood exploded outward, the creature gasped once, took a step back and slumped to the ground. It gasped again as trees bobbed in fury to a heaven-sent storm and fairies hummed an evil song.

Sherida watched the last breath leave the large cat and it collapsed, dead. She stepped back several feet, before releasing her breath.

Inhaling, she saw turtles swimming through blue clouds of soft wool and doves singing to the glory of the sun.

She collapsed shuddering and slept, dreaming of simpler times.

Half an hour later they slumped the still out of it Theodore onto Bill's couch.

"Trudy's still out, she'll probably be gone awhile." Bill closed the curtains.

"Have they got any credit cards?"

"Yup," Bill responded.

"Then they'll be gone for quite a while," the rest responded in unison.

"So what the hell is going on here?" Fred burped. "Oh man, one too many slices of pizza or beers."

Roger quickly filled him and Sam in on what had transpired the last few weeks as they all cracked open fresh beers. Bill added his story.

The two stared quietly after Roger was done talking. "Just so I get this straight. You think there's a hunk of this metal inside Sam and me?"

"Yes, and I think I can prove it. Bill, will you grab that metal detector we rented?"

"I'll get it, it's in the basement."

"You guys are nuts, totally frigging screwed. It's not possible. If I've a chunk of steel inside of me after all of these years surely I'd know," Sam said angrily.

Theodore stirred from his spot on the coach, shook his head and said quietly, looking more than a little ashen. "No, it's more than possible." He sat up, rubbed his face, looking like someone who'd woken up the morning after they've just lived through their worst nightmare. "I was hoping after it was out of me that this madness was over. I see now this is just the beginning of another phase. And I'm tired of denying the truth. I've been wrong," he sighed. Theodore reached into his coat pocket.

"You have it with you, don't you?" Roger whispered.

"Yeah, I have it. Gave me so many years of grief but I couldn't throw it away. One of the things I discovered was that I knew it had a purpose for being here and being in me. Perhaps tonight I discover why?"

Theodore removed the rag he'd used to wrap the shiny irregular shaped piece of metal and put it on the table. "I usually keep it locked away in my safety deposit box, but something told me to bring it here tonight after what you said Roger."

Fred picked it up. "It's just a hunk of metal. Take a look." He handed it to Sam.

"I ain't touching it. Probably got some of his guts and crap all over it. Can't be too careful what with AIDS, Covid and all that weird shit these days."

The others looked at him with their mouths agape.

Finally Roger spoke up. "That's lunacy, Sam. I can't believe you'd say something rude like that."

"Okay, I'm sorry."

"Here take a look at this." He got up and retrieved the other piece from where it sat on the mantel and set it on the table. "Fred, put the other piece just beside it and watch very closely. Bill's seen this, but Theodore you can also check this out."

Bill set down the bulky metal detector he'd rented for the occasion and stood around the small coffee table with the others.

For long seconds nothing happened.

"Wow, now that's pretty wild. Does either one of them begin to play the Star Spangled Banner or something? Or is this the whole show?" Fred frowned as he peered very intently at the two pieces and took a long pull from his can of beer.

"Maybe they're too far apart?" Bill said.

"Good point, I'll move it slightly closer." Roger reached out to bring the smaller piece closer but just before he could the sound of metal rattling on glass broke the silence.

"What the ..."

"It's starting," Theodore whispered and leaned closer. "I've had dreams and in them I kept seeing this piece merging with others, or at least wanting to." Roger watched as Theodore turned pale. He knew the man wasn't lying. Somehow, he knew and Roger knew he wasn't lying.

Roger pulled his hand back. The clink of metal on glass rose eerily. The smaller piece began to vibrate and shake. Then it jerked towards the larger piece.

"Christ!! Did you see that?" Fred exclaimed. "You've a freaking magnet in your hand don't ya!"

Roger simply lifted his hands, showed his palms to everyone and leaned back to sip on his beer. Again the eerie sound of metal dragging itself on glass commenced. Everyone stared intently as the smaller piece slid towards the larger fragment and with an audible click it locked itself into place.

Silence reigned for long seconds.

"Je-Zus," Fred finally said.

Theodore picked up the now larger piece of metal and scrutinized it. "There's no markings, no lines to tell where they just joined. For all intensive purposes it is one piece. Remarkable."

"Let me see," Fred scrutinized the glistening metal and tried prying it apart. "It ain't letting go."

"Whoa. Doesn't anyone find this just a bit freaky?" Sam pulled back into the confines of the couch.

"Nah, it's been done before," Bill said coolly. "I'm sure if we conjured up Houdini's ghost he'd tell us how this was done."

Roger glanced sideways at him. "Sure, Mr-it's-too-frigging-weird."

"Hey, I was a little high at the time. Could use a shot of the stuff tonight though, as my wife would say this is sure getting on my tits."

Fred scratched his head, "and you're trying to tell Sam and me that we've got a hunk of this metal inside of us."

"No way," Sam added, his face turning the color of January snow.

Theodore sat quietly turning the metal over in his hands. "I knew this would happen when Roger called for us to get together. I've had dreams about this happening."

"We'll soon find out. Bill, hold the metal detector up to Sam's stomach."

"No. You ain't getting that thing near me. Try Fred first. He's got a bit more flab to go through."

Bill held the awkward metal detector up to Fred's stomach nearly knocking over a vase in the process. No change in the number of beeps. "What the ..."

"Are you sure that thing works? Here, try me then." Sam said as he stood up. The same result as Bill.

"Thank goodness," Fred said, looking relieved. "You almost had me believing this crazy story."

"I don't get it. Why is there nothing inside them," Bill said, as he swung the detector over Fred's ring finger hand and it went crazy.

"Oh yes there is. I saw all six of us get touched by the light that night. I dreamt it a million fucking times." Theodore spat, as he grabbed the hunk of metal sitting on the table. "Unless ..." He held it under the metal detector. No change in the tone of the machine.

"Well, how does that work, when I had the metal detector at the airport going off like crazy?"

"Don't know. Unless the detector isn't strong enough, for whatever reason. Or alien metal maybe doesn't behave with any normal properties we know of?"

Theodore thought for a moment as he stared at the metal fragment in his hand. "Let's hold it up to Fred's stomach and see what happens. None of us knew it was in our bodies, maybe it only reacts to other pieces or know when it time is right to awaken. After all if it could move the metal across the table it can probably move it around in his body."

Fred's face turned pale. "Alien metal. No flipping way, I've seen this movie before. This is where it launches itself out of my guts and I die a grisly blood soaked death as lunch."

"Grab him boys," Roger said. They quickly wrestled the out-of-shape man to the ground. One lifted his shirt, while Roger held the object near his stomach where his scar was located on him.

Fred squirmed and began to holler.

"Shut up Fred, this won't hurt."

"How the hell do you know? Have you ever tried this before?"

"Has anyone ever tried this before?" Sam asked laughing, "Hey if anyone could use a few pounds less it would be you."

"Go to hell," Fred's eyes bulged out again and he continued his earlier struggles. "No matter what happens, you ain't cutting me open."

"Why, you've enough antiseptic in you to sterilize the wound."

"Beer isn't an antiseptic," Fred began to squirm again.

"Thanks, Sam. Look, Fred relax will ya. If this hurts we'll stop. Deal. Just no screaming or I'll have to whack you upside the head with this hunk and knock you out. Got it?" Theodore added.

Roger looked at Theodore and caught the rare streak of humor shining through. He was terrified but he could tell his old friend was secretly enjoying this. That was a relief, for a moment he thought they'd put him over the edge of sanity.

Fred finally he ceased his struggles and relaxed. Roger continued holding the metal object next to Fred's heaving stomach.

"See? Nothing's happening. Can we quit this stupid idea and get everyone off me?"

Sam snickered, "I'll bet it just takes longer to react, the man has a lot of insulation there."

"Fuck you," Fred replied. "Now can everyone get the hell off me?" He grinned. "What the ..." his face paled. "Ah, a cramp just there. Oh, again."

"What? What is it?" Theodore asked.

"Ah guys, look at this." Roger stared hard at surface of Fred's gut as twitching began to break its surface.

"What is it?" Theodore asked.

Fred blinked from a brief jolt of pain, "something's moving inside me. Like bad gas or food poisoning beginning and you can't control yourself." Another twitch, an audible grumble came from his midsection. "Hey guys, I saw Aliens and I don't like this one bit. Oh, there's definitely something moving. This is where I'm going to explode outwards, aren't I?"

"Relax Fred it's only metal, not an alien with bad attitude and a four movie contract."

A series of shudders broke the surface of his skin. A lump began to form under it and move towards the metal Roger was holding.

"That's it, I'm out of here," Fred shoved hard and pushed everyone over. "You guys are absolutely stir crazy." The metal fragment fell from Roger's hands and slid across the floor behind the couch.

As Fred rose the others simply stared dumbfounded. "What the hell is your problem?"

"Look Fred," gasped Roger. There, outlined against his stomach, was the shape of the metal piece inside Fred's body.

"Holy shit," Fred stared, holding his shirt aside. The object appeared to be straining against his skin, as if pushing from the inside out. Fred bent over in pain. "Ah, god."

"Now what do we do?"

"Get a knife," Sam said.

Fred's eyes opened in terror. "Like hell." He lowered his shirt and started to leave.

"Wait," Theodore said as Fred turned. "Did you just see that Roger?" Under the white cotton of his shirt a dull glow started.

Everyone stared as Fred slowly lifted his shirt again. There, on the surface of his skin, glowing metal spots began to form.

"Holy shit," everyone said at once.

"It's leaching itself through his skin," Theodore uttered as he stared. "Damn, no knife then?" he smirked.

They watched as the shimmering mercuric globules oozed past the surface of Fred's skin seeping into metallic pools and slowly re-solidifying into the dull metal piece they saw outlined against his skin.

The glowing stopped. The foreign metal object hung clinging to the outside of Fred's stomach. Theodore reached up to touch it and it fell away, sliding across the floor as if pulled by some unforeseen force. It rolled under the couch, where the larger piece lay. In the silence of everyone's breath the ominous click was deafening.

Seconds passed before anyone could move out of their catatonia.

"Did we just see what I thought I just did?" Everyone reached over and took a long sip of their beer. "Yup."

Finally, Theodore turned to Fred. "You okay?"

Fred nodded stupidly. "Well I've passed a lot of stuff in my time, gas mostly, but never heavy metal." He reached down and rubbed his stomach. "Damn that's the wildest experience I've ever had, well next to the threesome with Betty Fergusan and Margaret Jones the night of the school prom." His grin could beat out a Cheshire cat.

The other four burst out laughing, until tears streamed down their faces. They stopped laughing when Roger reached under the couch and put the metal object on the table. It had grown larger by the addition of the new piece. It was obviously nearly complete, needing what looked like only a couple more pieces.

"We know who's next." Everyone stared at Sam, whose laughter died in his eyes.

"It's okay Sam. It only tickled a little."

"Easy for you to say, I've got a wife and four kids to worry about. I doubt like hell my insurance would cover injuries caused by an alien piece ejecting from my body." Sam lifted his shirt. Roger held the object next to his body.

Like before, the object began to twitch under the surface of his skin after a few seconds. A glow began and metal spots appeared like mercury in composition. Only this time the mercuric globes puddled onto the piece that Roger held against Sam's stomach, flowing into the larger piece. The glowing stopped when an audible click was heard. Roger turned the larger piece over in his hands. "There's still no lines marking where the pieces joined together." He held it out to the others, they glanced and for the most part, simply took further sips, not wanting to remotely come close to touching the metallic object.

"Yeah, but wait a minute. It looks like there's still a piece missing," Fred said as he picked up the nearly circular object.

Roger stared, he was right. And he knew why.

"You guys realize that this is no ordinary hunk of metal. Nor was that night at the summer camp an ordinary night," Theodore piped up.

Fred, "Well, the beer was ordinary. Unless it had gone skunky and we never realized it."

Bill pondered, "Right, kids drinking off beer. We wouldn't know the side effects. Could be good grounds to sue on."

"Are you for real?" Theodore glared.

"Or like, we were implanted by ... by what, aliens?" Sam shook his head.

"I know you're having a hard time with this one Sam. But yes, we were." Theodore began, "I take it no one here has any memory of the night at the lake when we stole the case of beer and snuck away to the docks to drink it?"

They all shook their heads.

Bill spoke up, "I vaguely remember us running around drunk and one of us, I thought it was you Theodore, on the dock yelling something about ... lights, lights on the water."

"I'll have that beer now." Theodore took a long pull from his drink and ran his hands through his long hair before speaking. "We'd snuck down to the other side of the lake where the docks were," he began talking in a daze.

"Hey I remember that, I think it was Bud. The case of beer was Bud and I snuck it out of the Camp counselors' office," Fred interjected.

"Yeah, that's really important isn't it?" Roger shook his head.

"Well if you dislike Coors it is." Fred spate back.

"By the docks there was a spit of land where we could watch if anyone came, and take off if we had to. The night was clear but mist had begun to form on the lake. And loons, I remember the loons with their haunting cries, like they were warning us."

"Don't remember that," Fred added.

"We'd all had a beer or three each and were laughing our heads off, drunk as skunks. That's when Sam tried to light his first cigarette. He stuck the wrong end in his mouth and caught the filter on fire."

"Hey, I remember that, now." He rubbed at his lips. "Couldn't figure out why my lips were burnt for a few days."

"Don't remember that either," Fred frowned as he drank from his can of beer. "I remember the beer was Bud though."

"Yeah, the important stuff. I see by your gut it isn't suffering any withdrawals from that night," Bill snickered.

"Yeah. I call it deja-Bud," Fred laughed as he finished the can and crushed it in his hand.

"Well I began to get sick, I think it was the ..."

"Chili Con Carne," they all muttered.

"I think we had it nearly every bloody night that summer."

"Hey, remember the farting contests under the covers?"

They all laughed.

"Okay, serious now." Theodore broke in. "I remember the Chili. I ran into the woods to throw up. It was Sam that ran onto the dock after he burnt his lips. He was sprawled out flat on the dock trying to put water on his mouth. The others began to join him and started to shuck their clothes. The plan was we'd all go skinny-dipping after we worked up the courage. I started to walk back towards you guys when Sam yelled something about bizarre lights dancing under the water. In the mists I stopped near the edge of the trees, I couldn't see clearly. Then I saw the lights."

Fred burped and piped up, "Christ, I remember that now. I was standing on the dock, my shorts hanging around my knees, taking a piss, my pecker hanging out and the whole surface of the water began to erupt in chaos."

The others sat silently. Roger knew, like he, they were all pulling back dribs and drabs of memories they'd forgotten or were made to forget.

Theodore continued. "Yes, lights swirling like the Aurora Borealis. The mists heaved upward and something dark broke the surface of the water."

"I barely remember the lights, or anything after that."

The others agreed.

"I do," Theodore spat as the color drained from his face.

They all turned to face Theodore, sat down their cans, and waited as he worked up the nerve to continue.

"The rest has haunted me most of my life since. I crouched back under the bushes and watched, puke dribbling down my neck, in awe as the lights surrounded you guys and held you motionless. Then a being surrounded by brilliant white light rose from the hovering object, which by then I knew was a spacecraft, and walked slowly amongst you."

"The being in white, it was a she wasn't it?" Roger asked.

"Yes. I called her an angel; how'd you know?"

"I'll tell you later."

"She pulled away from the small ship and floated to the ground. Flowing platinum hair, a white uniform that looked like veils. Long veils that streamed behind her as she walked. She touched each of your foreheads and pulled something that glowed from a pouch on her side."

"The metal!" Roger spurted.

"Yes. She touched it against each of your midsections. I couldn't see what she was doing but now I know she was inserting the metal into your bodies. I dreamt it so many times."

"Hey wait a minute, though, you weren't on the docks. How'd you ...?"

"She looked around after she was done and seemed to peer at something on her arm, like a compass or something, and began to walk straight towards me."

"Jeezus."

"I tried to run, but couldn't. I was scared so shitless I couldn't make my legs move. I remember pissing myself in fear as she touched me with the metal and that's it, the rest went blank. I didn't start getting the dreams until many years later, nearly every night. I had the piece taken out of me, hoping that would stop the dreams, but it didn't." Theodore shook his head and slumped back on the couch, the look of haunt crossing his eyes. "It only awoke other things."

Roger simply stared at the metal on the table, as did the others.

"Wow, that's freaky," Bill muttered. "I'll never drink another Bud in the same light again."

"Whew, thought you were going to say you'd never drink another Bud again. Hey, could make a great TV ad though." Fred grabbed for another can and popped it open with a fizz.

"So who's missing then? I mean there's still what looks like a piece missing," Bill said as he turned the metal over in his hands.

"Mike Amberside. That's who."

"Who?" Fred scratched his head.

"Tall skinny kid, red hair. I think his parents were rather rich."

"Funny, that must have been erased from my mind too, don't remember him," Fred frowned.

"Obviously it isn't in your karma to remember anything, except the vitally important stuff," Theodore smiled at his friend.

"Yeah, like we were drinking Bud."

They all laughed.

"Yeah, but Mike's dead," Sam said.

"Thanks for the subtlety," Roger said softly. Recollections of the haunting sounds of squealing rubber, billowing clouds of acrid black smoke and white-haired angels with singsong voices dragging him away. The smell of burning rubber never seemed to leave his nose, nor the sound of exploding glass from his years of drunken adolescent stupidity, from his memory. "Yes, he's dead, car crash back in eighty-seven. I killed him. Couldn't drag him from the car in time," He lied. He couldn't tell them about the angel, they had barely accepted the truth about the metal, but to expect them to believe the same being was protecting him? Roger retreated to the other end of the room, and leant against the fireplace.

Sam was going to say something, but Fred elbowed him, "give him a moment." Theodore walked up to him, the others returned to watching the game that was on. "Sorry man, it's a shitty thing to have to deal with, but I'm curious. I was at your home visiting you the day after you got out. You couldn't walk, so how in hell did you escape from the wrecked car."

"You mentioned an angelic figure in white. That's how I knew it was a woman. If you can believe this, I think she dragged me from the car and has been keeping an eye on me since, and perhaps the others too for all we know, over the years. I call her my angel guardian. I'll tell you more later over coffee or something. Let's finish this, I'm getting tired."

The others sat, silent as the two rejoined the group. "So what happens now? Was all this bullshit we just went through for nothing?" Sam stood up, his face going red.

"Can it will you Sam. It's not Roger's fault Mike is dead. No offense buddy."

"None taken."

Theodore rose and paced the room. "Well the way I see it we can apply to have the body exhumed. Might take a few months, maybe a year or two, or longer. Or ..."

"Oh yeah I can see it now. Reason for exhumation – suspect piece of alien metal in body. I think we'd all be elected to go in for mental testing. I still think I should, I'm having a hard time swallowing all of this," Sam spat out.

"Well you saw it with your own eyes. There is another way," Roger said.

"Exactly!" Theodore turned from the fireplace he stood before. "We dig him up."

"We what!!" Fred and Sam gasped at the same time, spitting beer all over the carpet. "Oh, man my wife is going to kill me. Did you and the guys have fun playing poker? Nah, we decided to dig up a cadaver, seemed like a cool thing at the time." He wiped at the mess with his foot, soaking it up with his sock.

"I knew I should have stayed home that summer," Bill piped up. "Summer camp or Disneyland, I picked summer camp, thought I'd get lucky with Sally in the girls camp across the lake."

"You're one sick man. I ain't- -"

Roger thrust out his hand, "I'm in for digging up the body."

Theodore thrust his out and covered Roger's, "so am I."

Bill scratched his head. "Damn it, I've come this far."

The three turned and stared at Fred and Sam.

"Has anyone given this any serious thought? I mean, what if we put this thing together and something freaky happens, we get sucked into an alien world or wake up to some kind of alien death god. I've seen Stargate, this kind of thing always goes bad," Sam sputtered.

"Like it or not, we're already involved and we need to carry this through to the end. Whatever that end might be," Theodore spoke.

"I'll bet some bad ass chick. You remember that movie Amazons from Venus or planet of double D cup? They're all nymphos and they've screwed all the men there to death and came here looking for more men to breed with. Yeah, I'll bet one appears and says 'I'm your slave, take me'. I'm in. Besides, beats watching ET on TV." Fred covered the other hands.

"Crap, I'll bet all you do at night is sit around watching art movies."

"Pretty much, our relationship has evolved to the S and M stage."

"Cool."

"Yeah, she sleeps and I masturbate."

"Oh, not so cool."

"Fuck! I'll join in. But I'll only hold the flashlight and keep an eye out. I ain't going down into the hole and I sure as hell ain't doing any digging. Deal?" Sam finally said.

"Deal," the rest answered and Sam covered the rest of the hands with his.

"Next weekend, we'll start at the hangout, same time, same place. We'll probably need a couple of drinks to get started."

"Or something stronger," Bill smiled, "I'll bring a couple of spiffs of the green stuff."

For a long moment the five stared at each other and breathed deep. The enormity of what they were about to undertake sinking in.

Bill glanced over to Fred. "You never had a threesome with Betty Fergusan and Margaret Jones? What a cow that Betty is. I took her out on a couple of dates. She told me she was a virgin and didn't want to have sex before getting married."

Fred smiled, "Hey, yeah, just gotta have the knack. You know what they say 'It's not the size of the wand that counts. It's how well you beat the sides'."

"Or make the walls want to suck themselves in on your lovestick." Sam responded.

They all laughed as their hands separated.

When she awoke to the distant rumble of thunder that her senses told her it was real and not some delusion brought on by the drugs, Sherida scrambled to dig a hole in the soft earth with the broken talon. As the first dribbles began to filter through the trees in the small clearing she patted the soil over the covered animal. Before she thrust the talon at the beasts head as a grave marker she carved a symbol on her shoulder. A talisman tattoo carved from something of the defeated enemy and worn eternally to remember her defeated enemy and hold its power within her, a tradition on her world.

"You should have killed me when you had the chance."

Sherida rose and checked her timer, in ten more minutes the awaiting ship would beam her back up. She raced to the monument and grabbed the crystal on top of it as she heard the growl of another Pathess cracked the splatters of her tears and the planets rain somewhere in the background. Only softer in tone. "Looks like someone isn't getting their other half to cozy up with tonight and has begun to look for them."

Her body began to shimmer.

It was a beautiful day outside the museum. Roger groaned. He didn't believe he had let himself get roped into taking the kids to the museum on a golfing day. Right about now he and Bill would be teeing off and tomorrow the gang had set up as the night to go to the graveyard. "Okay kids, we're here, let's do the family bonding hour and enjoy this museum."

"Yeah, you're the greatest, Dad." They screamed and took off into two different directions.

He tried to whisper 'stop' but it was too late as they disappeared into different rooms. He'd go after young John, at least he knew where he would be. Roger entered the room with the dinosaur exhibits. Like most young boys his son was nuts over dinosaurs. "How can you get excited about something sixty million years old," Roger muttered. He spotted his son staring up at a large skeleton. "Johnny, haven't I told you that you shouldn't go running around in a public place." Roger began to scold his son as he grabbed his hand and yanked him away from the display. "What if that thing should break apart and hit you or crush you." Now he was sounding like Beth.

Roger stopped and stared at the display for a moment letting his son's hand slip from his grasp. 'Stractusaurus', it said. 'Plant-eating dinosaur from Jurassic period'. Yet something looked oddly familiar about that dinosaur's skeleton.

A crash alerted Roger to the fact that Johnny had slipped his grasp and knocked over a garbage can behind him.

Roger turned and caught his younger daughter darting from the room. She must have been hiding behind the garbage can. Johnny stood there with the look of angels in heavenly bliss. "Ashley did it."

"No. I didn't." Came the reply from around the corner as she peaked her head in.

"Ashley, in this room right and come clean up this mess. That includes you young man as well."

Roger decided to ask the pointless question every parent asks in their lifetime when dealing with children and never learns, unless they have backup video or cellphone evidence, the answer to "who did this?"

They both looked at their dad and repeated the oft-used phrase, "She/he did it."

"It wasn't me Dad, it was John."

"No, Dad, Ashley did it."

"Liar. You did it." One began pushing the other.

"I don't care who did it. I want both of you to clean it up."

As they did, with much pushing and shoving, Roger glanced back at the skeleton. "Something vaguely familiar about that skeleton," he muttered as he walked from the room.

Chapter Nine

Supper done Roger sat out in his backyard, enjoying the fresh air. Sparky was busy chewing away on the large bone Roger had carried home the other night. He'd managed to gnaw his way through a tenth of it so far. Probably have half left for his next generation to chew on.

Johnny came running into the backyard. "Dad, Ashley pushed me."

His daughter came running in next, "he pushed me first Dad."

"Can't you two ever cut it out and play nicely with each other."

They both stopped their ribbing for a moment. "What ya doing Dad? You watching Sparky chewing on his dinosaur bone?" Johnny asked.

"On what? His dino? Just because that bone is large it doesn't mean it belongs to a dinosaur, son. They died off millions of years ago."

"See I told you, silly." Ashley ribbed her brother.

"Well, not that one. He's an old timer," he replied and pushed her.

"Cut it out you two."

"But Dad, Johnny said it was a dinosaur bone." Ashley put her hands on her hips and pouted.

"Well, it looks like a bone from that dinosaur in the museum," Johnny said.

"Son, we all have bones in our bodies and they all look the same, only that dinosaurs were a lot bigger. Besides, dinosaurs lived long before man was even around on this planet. In fact mammals weren't even around in dinosaur time."

"Told you so, silly." She was about to push her brother again.

"Did not."

"Hey take it to your mother," Roger yelled. "I came out here to get a little peace and quiet."

As they scampered off Roger stared at Sparky's bone. One thing was certain, his son was right. It sure look eerily like the bones from the dinosaur on display.

"No, pal, you don't seem to understand. They've restricted all access to information regarding the company. I can't help you today but if you leave a business card I'll have them contact you." The guard replied.

Tom wasn't about to do that. They said no contacts, and his guts told him something wasn't right here. This was a setup of some sort, maybe a decoy. He stared at the guard, needing something right about then to settle his nerves, but with the heightened security at the airports these days he didn't dare bring any coke or even any bud with him. "Here's my card."

He whipped out a wad of money. He snapped five hundreds down on the desk. "Does this help to jog your memory?"

"Works for me." The guard's eyes widened. Without cleaning his fingers of the chocolate remains of the doughnut he'd been enjoying, he stuffed the money into his pocket, then printed off a page from the computer. "This is everything we have on file regarding these guys and you never saw it before."

"Thanks." Without looking at the piece of paper Tom stuffed it into his briefcase and walked out. He needed at least a drink. He would have preferred a line and a hot blonde, but a drink would do for now. His head throbbed from the lack of coke. Time to score some in one of the local pubs.

"Hi Mike, long time no see. We hate to disturb you but we decided to stop by for a drop-in visit, literally. I see if you're still as good looking as ever after all these years," Bill said, as he stood in front of Mike Amberside's tombstone.

Fred gave him a playful shove, "hah, very funny."

"Okay guys, cut the clowning around, its past midnight and we've a body to dig up." Sam threw down shovels for the other four. They stared long and hard at the spades and the ground before them. To talk about digging up a body was one thing, to do it was another.

"Crap, we're not really going through with this, are we?" Bill grimaced as he handed out rubber gloves to everyone.

"What are these for?" Fred asked.

"So we don't leave fingerprints or any kind of DNA evidence behind."

"DNA on dirt?" Sam snickered. "I think you've been watching too many reruns of CSI."

"Hey, I agree with Bill. I've seen them get DNA off a dead mosquito that the killer swatted at." Fred smirked before he burst out laughing and the others joined in.

"We've already discussed this as a group." Theodore grabbed one of the shovels and slammed it into the ground. He put on the gloves, "at least it will keep dirt from getting under our nails."

"Holy shit, he's actually going to do it!" Bill gasped.

"Not he, it's we, now let's get digging." Fred threw down the sack he was carrying and emptied it out. "And give me a pair, hate to wreck my manicure." He stared at his blunt half chewed nails.

"What the hell is that stuff?" asked Roger, "and what the hell is that god-awful smell."

"Hey if we're talking aliens, we're talking possible vampires. I ain't taking no chances. This is garlic and I've brought a necklace of the stuff for everyone," Fred said, as he sorted the pile of wooden stakes, strings of garlic, crosses, plastic water pistols and mirrors. "Anything is possible, I'm take no chances."

Sam just shook his head. "No thanks, I'll take my risks with the aliens."

Roger glanced at the water pistols. "I get the rest of this stuff, but what's in the water pistols?"

"Water. Holy water."

"Where the hell did you get holy water from?"

"Stole it from the church."

"You stole holy water? Isn't that just a little sacrilegious? I mean wouldn't that wipe out the idea of purity?" Sam replied.

"Well, I couldn't very well say, 'Hey Pastor can I charge a gallon of Holy water onto my Visa? Just need it for a little protection from vampires, you know, for this dead guy we're digging up that we think has a hunk of alien metal in it. Vampires, you know, very weird people, can't tell what they'll eat next especially when they've been out of it for a few years. Wink, wink,'" Fred exasperated.

"Where the hell did you get the idea of sticking it into Super Soakers?"

"I watched the Lost Boys video last weekend. Sure zapped those baddies on tv."

"Fred, I'm not sure who's crazier here. You or the rest of us," Theodore added as he began to dig in earnest. The rest joined in until only the constant chunk of digging filled the air. Soon the four of them stood deep in the hole they'd dug, nearly over their heads. Sam stood on guard at the top waving about with a couple of flashlights. He'd agreed to be part of the group, but had no intention of being in the hole when they got to the body.

Mist rose from the sweat pouring off them. The air was still.

"What was that?"

"I think I hit the casket," Theodore replied and dropped to his knees. He felt around in the cold earth. "Yes it's the lid of the casket that we're standing on.'

"Shit!" yelled Fred.

"What's wrong?"

"I think I broke another nail," he said, as he held his hand.

"Can I beat him into a pulp with this shovel?" Roger looked at the other two in the hole.

Minutes later Theodore cleared aside the dirt from the top of the casket. It was hinged and they didn't want to expose more than needed. "Okay ready?"

Everyone nodded.

"You sure you don't want to see this?" Roger called up to Sam. "Could take a few great pictures on your cellphone.

"No thanks, I have no intention of viewing a dead body. I threw up at the sight of my son being born, and when I had to pull the neighbors' cat out from under my car after it got stuck in the radiator fan. No fucking way and the last thing we want is any kind of evidence that we've done this." Sam replied down at them.

"Just give a second." Fred opened his sack and threw a string of garlic around his neck, tucked the ornate cross into his pants, slung one super soaker over his head and trained two water pistols at the coffins lid. "Okay, I'm ready for anything the underworld can throw at me. Call me the White version of Blade, The Vampire Hunter."

"Are you for real?" Theodore blinked in disbelief, heaved and cracked the lid open. A thick hiss of air escaping filled the freshly dug pit. "Well we're in luck it appears to be airtight still. Which should mean no maggots at least."

"Maggots! Fuck! That smell." Bill covered his nose. "I think I'm going to be sick." His face turned green as he lurched over and retched his guts out.

"Sam, shine some more light down here where we can see something and here, spray some of this." Fred pulled out two cans of aerosol from his vest pocket and covered his face. "Crap, not in my face with the light."

"Sorry, but it smells horrid," Sam uttered as he tried to cover his nose and juggle the flashlights. "Hell, smells worse than a dead guy... Oh, sorry it is a dead guy. Didn't mean to insult you Mike."

"Get down here and take a whiff. Wow, didn't know how nasty this stink would be." Theodore grabbed one of the cans. "What is it?"

"Like Nilodor, only organic."

"Organic?" Roger asked.

"Yeah, organic. Need to be environmentally conscious these day." Fred smiled.

"But he's dead," Theodore shook his head and sprayed the can into the casket and the pit until the can emptied. "Well, that's the best idea you had all night. Now it smells like freshly squeezed oranges in here."

"And environmentally safe, too." Everyone snickered.

Theodore lifted the lid the rest of the way. They shone the light into the casket.

Everyone leaned forward, hands over noses. Except Bill, "I think I'm going to be sick again." He leaned back and started gagging.

"Great, now it smells like fresh puke in here as well."

"Holy! He looks like a frigging Nosferto stand-in," Roger uttered.

"Jesus!" Fred gasped. "Sam, quick, throw me down a stake and a hammer." He whipped a cross from his belt and held it before the body.

The body of Mike Amberside had shrunken and his gums had retracted exposing his teeth in an eerie death grimace. His hair and nails were long as well.

"Knock it off, Fred. After someone dies they lose their body fluids, which add up to nearly half their weight, and their hair and nails can keep growing for up to two years. Hence the belief that sprang up in the 1700's that men turned into vampires," Theodore spouted matter of factly.

"He's handy to have around. A bleeding Mr. Dictionary and Wikipedia all rolled into one. Do you do any magic tricks? Could be the next Houdini as well," Fred frowned.

"Yeah, right, just another urban legend. Seen it on that daft TV show." Sam threw down the stake and hammer. "The rest of us just normally watch reality TV."

"Or the Playboy Channel. Now there's reality."

"Can I flatten him with the back of my shovel?" Theodore asked, he'd been quite used to the gangs ribbing of his knowledge over the years.

"You believe what you will, I ain't taking any chances. I get a little squeamish at the idea of sucking your guys' necks and drinking your blood. Hell, I already told you I passed out when my son was born and get ill at the sight of Bloody Mary's and pizza sauce."

Fred moved around to the other side of the casket. "So you go right ahead and find the metal. I'll take no chances with Mr. I-look-like-a-Dracula-stand-in."

Roger looked at Fred strangely, while Bill continued to throw up as he got a whiff of the vile aroma wafting up occasionally from the casket.

Fred pulled a new pair of rubber gloves from his back pocket, he torn his old ones.

Bill stared in disbelief. "I thought you were a diesel mechanic. You've got nicer fingernails than my wife."

"I am and we're called diagnostic technicians these days. All the guys use them. They're non-latex, powdered and have special grip on the inside."

"Small wonder they aren't floral scented as well, do they come in decorator pastel shades for the discriminating auto-technicians?" Theodore smirked, getting one back.

"Okay, knock it off, I get the idea."

Theodore ripped the suit aside and there, against the hardened, shriveled skin was the outline of the object they knew would be there. He reached into his pocket and pulled out a switchblade.

"I'll make an incision and pull out the fragment. There'll probably be a hiss of gas being released. Bill, if you have anything left that hasn't been puked up, stand back."

As Theodore predicted, the sound of escaping gas filled the tense air. A gasp came from Mike's lips as his mouth opened. Fred jumped in shock. "He's waking up, we've disturbed the undead." Before anyone could stop him he slammed the hammer into the stake driving it into Mike's heart. Another groan of gas broke past Mike's lips. "Die blood sucker." He thrust the stake deeper.

"Will someone get the wannabe vampire hunter to mellow out? It was only gas," Theodore said as he struggled contain his stomach and fight back the frantic Fred. "Now give me a minute to pull back the hardened folds of skin."

Fred blasted Mike's face with the holy water as he stood up. "He could be right. No sizzling of evaporating flesh. Sorry. But I wasn't taking any chances."

"Sure I can't take just one swing at him?" The skin cracked and broke away revealing the piece of metal as Theodore pulled it free. The fragment gleamed in the light, untarnished. "Holy, it hasn't rusted or stained or anything." Roger said. "Okay, let's get out of here and cover him up."

Bill lurched again. "Give me a second, didn't think there was anything left inside to heave. Could use something to wash taste out of my mouth." He looked down at the super soaker and twisted off the end before rinsing his throat and spitting it out.

"Hey careful with that stuff, don't know what side effects drinking Holy water would have."

"It's just bloody water that someone waved a cross over. Man, you lead to get a sheltered life."

"Wow," Roger said, "I've never seen that much come out of someone before. Have you got anything to eliminate puke breath for the ride home?"

"Yeah, got some sugar free mints in the car."

"Sugar frigging free?"

"Yeah," everyone replied in unison. "Don't want to get any extra calories in your diet."

Just as the sun was beginning to crack the cover of darkness, they patted down the new section of sod they'd brought along.

"Damn, except for the new edges, you'd never know."

"Got it covered." Fred pulled two aerosol cans from his sack. "It's forest green spray paint; they use it in greenhouses to enhance the look of plants." He tossed one at Sam. The bits of dirt blended away as they sprayed.

Sam glanced at the side of can, "Just checking to make sure it's biodegradable as well." The rest snickered.

"Wow. You'd never know. Okay let's hit the showers at Bill's and grab some of those brewskis in the fridge."

As they drove to Bill's silence filled the van. Each with their own thoughts. Roger realized through all of this Theodore had managed to find humor and humanity again. He seemed to be right in his element, like Holmes on the prowl.

"Did you guys catch his suit?" Fred muttered.

"How tacky. Did we all dress like that in the seventies?"

"Nah, just Mike, he never was a sharp dresser."

"Definitely no fashion sense."

Another long pause. Sam tapped Fred on the shoulder. "You didn't really have a threesome, did you? Was it good?"

Fred smiled, "It was amazing. Best part, after I got off..."

"Which, Mr. Quick Draw McGraw was about eight seconds."

"Piss off, I lasted a few minutes." They all chuckled. "The best part, the two of them went at it for a couple of three hours. It's amazing how many orgasms women can have. It's like they have this automatic rewind or you put the batteries into the Ever-ready bunny backwards."

"You what?" Theodore grimaced, not getting it.

"It keeps coming and coming, instead of going." Fred snorted.

Sam looked up in dismay. "Is sex all you think about?"

Fred. "Pretty much."

Bill frowned. "Threesome, yup that'll be on my bucket list."

Tom lay in his bed at the hotel room. The cards sat in a pile on the night-table beside him. The sheet of paper the guard had given him didn't provide much more information then he already knew, except for an emergency contact number and another address in the industrial part of town. Tom had driven there and found the same deal; big warehouse, empty, with only a desk and a dead phone line. He'd checked with the land office and Unearthly Creations had paid the taxes and rent for the year.

Nothing here made sense. He was missing something, but what? It had been a long and fruitless day.

He picked up the stack of cards that Unearthly Creations had sent him and stopped when he came to the one of the couple in the bedroom. The man, his hands tied to the bedposts. A brunette, running an ice cube down his trembling stomach, tormenting him. Another card showed a redhead, her head turned sideways, in obvious enjoyment of the male atop of her, driving into her again and again. The sensations, surrounding him, so real, he blinked one moment the male, the next the female. This was one step past virtual sex. Tom smirked. The one of two guys alone in a tent on a camping trip did nothing for him. But this one ...

The sheer thrill on the woman's face as she's thrust against a brick-wall under a bridge, traffic speeding overhead, while the male pressing up behind her enters. A couple sitting cross-legged, her on top of him, tantric sex at its finest, incense filling the air. He was lost in a harem scene. A woman in bondage; the eroticism of this one definitely did something to Tom. Maybe it was the bondage he felt inside, the bondage of illusions, his reality, his soul. He laughed. He'd read somewhere that the eyes are the greatest deceivers.

But his favorite fantasy, the one he'd played out in real life, was a ménage a trios. Perhaps that was it. The ultimate turn-on, two women turning each other on and then turning him on. He placed the cards on the night-stand and shut off the lights. In the darkness the crack of a whip, the groans of a man struggling in his bonds.

Tom spun in the dark, the brunette is untied. She fell to her hands and knees, the blonde putting one black stiletto boot forward. Red lipstick smeared the tip as the brunette began kissing the end. Hunger and need too obsessive in her eyes, pleasuring her mistress. Lost in the madness of desire, the want to give pleasure to her that dominated her, controlled her. That was it, wasn't it?

He stiffened at the creak of a door. He was dreaming now. This had never happened, something new entering his view in the card. But he wasn't holding a card. He turned away from the moans of the blonde as her slave's lips rose higher across hot flesh. Domination and control. Needing to satisfy her mistress.

Tom walked to the door and opened it. Another apartment, he walked in. It was his place. Hearing the cries of the blonde, he turned to look back into the bedroom. Empty. Odd.

He walked around his apartment. No one there. He switched on the stereo, hating silence and being alone. Your fears are what control you, he'd read.

He feared being alone, yet he'd remained single his whole life. Walking that danger's edge. Still he enjoyed the thrill of being single; money brought with it many pleasures, booze, drugs, and gorgeous women. There wasn't much he couldn't buy. Always finding desperate women, wanting to get rich in modeling, or to find a rich man, their white knight.

Static came out of the stereo, he tried the TV but it was the same. Tom spun frantically around, sweat breaking on his forehead. This was too eerie.

The dread followed him as he stepped out of his apartment, the dread that he existed in a world with no one else. He walked over to the apartment three doors down. Samantha would be home.

They'd spent much time together, using each other for company and sex. Sometimes she'd bring a friend and the three of them would have a great time. Tom pressed the buzzer. It didn't work. Out of curiosity he tried the door, and it swung open.

"Samantha?"

He walked in. She always locked her door. The taste of dullness ached in his throat, knowing, fearing she wasn't here.

"Samantha?" he yelled louder, worried.

No one. He advanced through the apartment, the inky pit widening inside him. Threatening to fall in. He ran back into the hallway and slammed the door, his chest heaving, sweat beading his brow, and stared. Yawning before him, stretching as far as he could see, apartments, their doors all open. "No."

He entered another apartment, and there in the empty room stood a knight's full armor. He reached to open the visor. The moans of the bound man and the brunette. Tom stepped back, behind the visor his face, locked in a state of sheer pleasure, leering, stoned on physical pleasure. The suit of armor tottered and fell forward, pulling him into it.

Tom woke in a sweat. "God." He glanced over at the clock. 3:58 a.m.

"Illusions," he cried out as he sat up. How realistic could they make these cards? What if ...

What if they could produce something bigger than cards? He got up to get a glass of water. What if ...

He swallowed the water and stared into his reflection in the mirror. What if they can set up a whole scene, like the building and the empty floors? No, that's sci-fi crap.

A wave of nausea hit him. "What the ..."

He glanced at the clock. This was LA. A prelude to an earthquake? The disorientation passed. "Okay, maybe just my nerves," He said aloud for comfort, realizing he'd not eaten anything since lunchtime. "Maybe I shouldn't be drinking on an empty stomach."

He left his night light on as he fell asleep, this time

Four of them staggered around in the living room. Fred snored away in the corner, mouth open where'd he'd fallen asleep. Roger was the last to climb out of the shower built into the next room. Bill had arranged to have the weekend alone and the guys over to play one of their famous all-night poker games.

"Okay, someone wake up Fred. Everyone's showered, had a coffee or two. I've got both video cameras on. One set to take an image every two seconds and the other to run on constant. The video machine has the digital ready to record. Are we set?"

They all sat down around the coffee table on which sat the larger piece of metal.

"Knock your socks off," Sam growled. "I'd have preferred to have played poker myself. This had better be good. UFO crap. Let's do it, I've only got about two hours left before I gotta go. Promised the kids I'd take them to the matinee and not a wink of sleep, yet."

Roger unwrapped the smaller piece and set it at the other end of the table. Theodore checked the time "6:58 AM." He turned everything on.

They stared at the two objects for long moments. Fred began to slump over, his snoring breaking the silence. Roger nudged him awake again. "Can it will ya. Can't pick up anything on the audio with all that damn snoring."

Theodore moved the smaller object closer until it was only about a foot away. "Okay it was about there that we got a reaction out of the other pieces. I'd have thought that the bigger chunk would have greater pull," he mused.

Again they sat waiting. Nothing happened.

"Well this is beginning to look like a crock of shit."

Roger leaned over and was about to push the smaller piece closer when it began to vibrate, clinking on the glass. He took his hand away in alarm. The clinking stopped.

"Okay," Theodore turned the one camera on Roger, "just reach out like you're going to move the piece and let's see what happens."

Roger did and the metal began to shake again.

"I'm curious. Bill you try that and see what happens."

Bill reached over and nearly touched the metal. Nothing. Theodore had everyone else try it with the same results except snoring Fred.

"Well it looks like Roger, for whatever reason, is our man."

Theodore also grabbed his cellphone, as did a couple of the others and hit movie to record what was about to happen.

"I kinda feel like Arthur as he goes to pull Excaliber from the rock." Roger reached over and pushed the smaller fragment closer. It shook, clinking all the way until the piece pulled itself against the larger one and everyone took a breath in. Except for Fred, head slumped back on the couch, still fast asleep.

An audible clink echoed to the silence.

They all waited breaths held as the now complete fragment sat there looking for all the world like a normal piece of oval shaped stainless steel. Theodore moved slowly around the room with his cellphone, hoping for something to happen.

The seconds ticked by. Some exhaled, scratched at various body parts, yawned quietly. Others glanced at their watches, yawning again.

Silence.

The faint click of the video camera broke the stillness, then Fred let out a loud snort. "That's it," Sam jumped up. "I've had enough of this craziness, I'm not sitting here any longer listening to fat Fred sounding like a mating call of three drunk elephants. I don't see shit happening. I'm tired, cranky and hungry. I'm going home while I can still get an hour of sleep in." He clicked off his cellphone's camera and got up.

"Hang on a minute Sam, let's check outside and see if there's been any unusual sightings in the sky tonight. I've a friend at the international airport who's on duty." Bill blurted out, trying to get Sam to stay.

Sam grabbed his jacket. "To think I risked my life and career for this bullshit. Fuck this noise, I've had enough and I'll say this. Sooner or later, the cops might open an investigation into the digging up of Mike's body. We all agree to keep our mouths shut. No snitches," Sam stormed out of the house.

Roger rose to go after him.

"Let him go, Rog. He's tired, as we all are. I think we should call it a night after we check the news." Theodore sounded disappointed. All the dreams and nightmares he'd had, all boiled down to this moment.

They checked the news; nothing. Bill's friend at the control tower reported the same thing. A quiet normal night.

As they began packing up Roger looked at the metal ovoid. "Hey, I thought the surface of this thing couldn't be scratched," he muttered.

Theodore came over. "I did try years ago and couldn't manage it?"

"Well I also did try the other night to take a knife and mark the edge before we finished with the last piece and couldn't leave even a faint mark. But look at these marks, almost look like some caveman's scratches or something. I don't recall seeing these on any of the parts before we joined it together."

"Not unless it was on the last one we got from Mike and I didn't look that closely at that section." Theodore stared as he lifted the round metal and showed it to the camera's eye. "Yeah, unusual, like petro glyph markings. Roger can you do a zoom in on the video?" He grabbed a Swiss army knife and tried to scratch the surface, to no avail as Roger zoomed in with his camera.

As Roger did so, Theodore frowned. He pressed harder and with a chink, both watched the blade break into two.

"Yeah, breaks the darn blade and no mark. That thing is like a stainless alloy of some kind."

"So what exactly is this made of?" Roger asked as he focused the video camera on the scratches.

"Not sure, yet something about those marks looks vaguely familiar. Can I take the tapes home and check something out?"

"Yeah go for it. I'll hang on to the metal."

"And I'll get some sleep. What a night," Bill muttered, stumbling back into the couch as he turned off the TV, too tired to care.

"Did I fall asleep? What happened? I dreamt an alien ship landed and took us to a planet full of gorgeous women," Fred blinked his eyes awake.

"Then you had more action than the rest of us. Let's call it a night."

"No, I mean really, what happened?"

"You know Fred, I don't think you're ready for the truth yet and I still don't get how you managed to get a threesome going with Betty Ferguson and Margaret Jones."

Fred smiled as he walked to his car. "Well, let me tell you about it."

Theodore just shook his head as he got into his car and sat quietly as the others drove off. I've seen them before, somewhere. They look vaguely familiar. He didn't want to say anything to Roger or the rest of them; at least not until he was sure, not until he'd had a chance to examine the data again. They'd already had too much disappointment tonight. Overhead the moon hung in the early morning sky, looking as it always did.

"Yeah," he whispered into the cool of the night as he rolled down his window. Don't know what or how to explain it. But something is different, something has changed, shifted. I can sense it. I don't know how, but we've done something by...? He drove along peering ahead, but not thinking about the road. It is intangible, one of those can't quite put my finger on it. Odd moments, but I know I experienced a sensation of some sort as the last part connected. "Now, to prove it and find out what."

Rain. Splattering by her ear, onto the newsprint stirred Sherida. Raining, memories of when she was seven, the gentle pitter-patter of rain hitting her parents' roof on the Tresuvian plains of her homeland. How often she'd listened to that sound, it used to put her to sleep at night during the hot humid summers before she left.

Her last memories of her parents and of being a child. Before she joined the Federation and became one of the angels. She smiled, so little left of her personal memories, nearly all were wiped clean in the training, they warned her, but like all that become angels, Sherida agreed. It was the most incredible experience she could ever hope to have in her lifetime and it had been until now. Along with the cyboratic equipment installed in her body, she knew also Beta-blockers kept her from having deep sleeps filled with any kind of dreams. Tears streamed down her face. She hadn't dreamed like this in many years.

The rain hitting the roof of her room, clanging on the metal and a familiar acrid aroma. Only this sound was slightly different and as suddenly as the rain started it stopped with a spurt and a grunt. Grunt?

Sherida shook her head, paper rattled, trying to get the fuzziness out of it. A rancid smell hit her. She opened her eyes and, from under the corner of the newsprint, caught sight of a worn out running shoe. A thin rubbery material next to the shoe caught her eye. Her senses detected male reproductive material inside of it. What the?

Heat, warmth, ran down the paper and something liquid puddled on the ground before her. Not ozone rich like the sweet summer rain back home. No, this was fouler, more acrid like ...

Ammonia.

"Damn!" she yelled as she stood up, flinging the paper aside. Memories of her mom, her home, the fight, her need to recuperate, and passing out under the newsprint came flooding back to her.

"Sweet Jesus!" A derelict exclaimed, interrupted in the act of trying to do up his fly. He took off up the alley pushing his shopping cart as fast as he could.

She flexed her arms and legs. Other than a little stiffness she was okay, her body had done well to repair itself. The bleakness of her situation sunk in. She glanced at her Earth Timer and realized she'd been out two days. "Two days? I've been out for two days? What I wouldn't give for a shower and one without any NH3 particles in it." She sniffed at herself. Sweat and urine resonated.

"So, now what? No established procedures or protocols for a situation like this." She closed her eyes and searched her memory banks, recalling all the training she had downloaded into her. "Nothing. There's the other eleven angels, except I've just destroyed the only tool that I might have been able to contact them. Without that I've have no knowledge of where on this planet they'd be and nor will they know where I am or if any of us were still alive. By Rama and Zarathustra, now what?"

Sherida smiled. Odd, it had been a long time since she'd uttered a natural curse. The last time was from her childhood. She sighed thinking about all the training and what it took to get her here. Some of the trials, tribulations and the excitement. Well, lady that you've got in buckets, the need for excitement. A tear streaked her cheek as she bent her head down. If only she could be home now, safe in her mother's arms. It had been so long, she couldn't barely recall what her mom looked like.

She wiped at it and stared. It had been the first time since she'd become part of the angel corps that she'd showed any emotion and weakness. They'd trained her not to dwell into weakness. Weakness brought indecisiveness and ultimately failure. Perhaps destroying the communicator and some of the controls of the implant within her, also destroyed some sort of emotional field dampening device.

She sighed again. To be home, not a zillion parsecs from nowhere, being hunted. "No, I must focus on why I'm here." Now she understood why the implants suppressed her emotions. It was so much harder to focus on what was important, like her assignment.

"Roger." She had to check to see how close he was and if he was safe. Sherida shook her head. Her emotions seeping through, more tears threatened. Trying to stay alive and figure out how to get back should be the logical course of action. She stared up at the single sun in the sky. And hope I'm not stranded here for the rest of my life?

Tom walked into the tall skyscraper again, just off Broadway. If the cards were illusion somehow this had to be also. There was something with the entire set up that stank of wrongness. It didn't make sense. Deceptions, he was good at deceptions, it was his job. It was how I made my livelihood. What if they could magnify the field of the cards and this was all illusion? Would it be that much harder to make me think I'm in an entire floor or talking to a real person when I thought I was just flying like an eagle or standing on a mountain top?

He walked past the guard, same black man, and glanced down at the desk. Same box of doughnuts, same paper. Tom's heart pounded a little louder as he stood waiting for the elevator. He noted that the security guard hadn't even acknowledged him. Surely he'd at least smile at the stranger that gave him more money than he probably made all week. Yeah, but then he was pretty rude yesterday. He stepped in and leaned against the back wall. Was it possible? Was this all a fantastic 3D illusion? I don't think they'd expected me to return or did they? The bell dinged, robot-like he strode out and walked down the hall. Tom swallowed twice and tried the ornate door belonging to Unearthly Creations. This is crazy thinking. Things like this just didn't really happen, did they? This corridor eerily like the one in his dreams. He'd had a bad dream, that was all, a bad dream. As Tom walked over to the cubicle emptiness and cobwebs answered his echoing footsteps. He turned around to stare at the sunlight streaming in. Behind him he spied the single set of footprints he'd just made. No others were there in the dust. He slowly walked around the elevator shaft, there should have been a second set, but wasn't.

Was it possible that this was a setup? A cover? Every time I entered one of the cards, it was new, no trace of the last visit. So nothing had changed, the guard hadn't recognized me. Or had it? Did I enter some sort of field generator and get put into another version of the cards and not know it. What a better way to trap someone or fool them.

He stared at the phone, a steady green light glowed back.

Tom stared again.

Something had changed, that light was red before. I'm sure of it. Maybe this was all in his mind, he was driving himself crazy. The trouble with good illusions was that you never knew when you were in that thin line between reality or something else. Like when I'm really high, although thank God I've never wanted to jump off a roof and fly when I'm stoned. There, he was spouting off garbage again. Maybe it was simply the paranoia generated by too much dope. He made a mental note, less Mary Jane and more coke or hash. Tom breathed deeply. He picked up the receiver and heard the buzz of a dial tone. So what had changed? Why was there a dial tone now?

"Okay, so let's try the emergency number." He reached into his briefcase and pulled out the sheet the guard had given him yesterday.

Three rings, then a slight change in tone indicating that the automatic answering machine had kicked in. "You've reached Unearthly Creations. Our office is now closed. If you'd like to leave a message do so at the beep."

Their agent Sherida had said not to contact them, what if she merely wanted not to be cut out of the picture? He waited a moment. Damn it, go with my gut instincts.

Tom left his name and office number he pausing, whispers, in the background whispers and ... Moans, it sounded like the moans of the two women. He pulled the receiver from his ear and listened again. Silence. Had I just heard that? He stared at the receiver in his hand. The faint crack of a whip. He put the phone back to his ear. It was coming from the phone!

He slammed down the receiver and glanced at his watch, he had only four hours to make it to the airport, get rid of the rental and clear security. He wanted to chat with the guard. Yet he sensed what he needed to do here was now done. He opened the pack of gum that was in his pocket and began to chew it. Gum?

He reached under the edge of the desk. It was gone, or rather, there wasn't anything there to start with. Oh yeah, I've been duped, taken royally, anally and I bloody fell for it.

Chapter Ten

Theodore had been studying the videotape with Roger for the last hour. There was something there, there had to be. Last night after he got home was the first time in years that Theodore had slept soundly. No haunting nightmares about aliens taking him away to their ship and performing bizarre experiments on him. Just sleep. Good old sleep.

He slowed down the video. The scratches he saw were indeed not there before the two pieces merged, but appeared on the surface of the two chunks as they joined together.

Theodore blinked as he caught sight of something odd. He replayed on slow mode again. It was there, almost like a blur or dimming as the two final pieces merged.

Theodore rewound the tape again, this time he hit freeze frame just at the moment the scratches began to appear. A ring of discoloration surrounded the metal.

He rewound it again. This time he caught another frame of picture in freeze frame. And the blur was there, only bigger like an expanding blob of gas.

Again Theodore rewound the tape and this time printed the image on his computer. He did this several times, until he caught several different frames on print. Then he sat down and arranged the pictures in timed order. Whatever it was it happened in less than the blink of an eye.

Theodore flipped the pictures like the images sometimes put into children's books to simulate a moving image.

Something burst from the metal at the exact moment the two final sections merged and that something expanded outward like a ripple in time. Just like a …

He sat dumbfounded.

Just like a signal, there had to be no other explanation.

Theodore returned to one of the printed pictures and stared at the scratches. He'd seen something like those before. But where?

Theodore picked up several of his books on older cultures and glimpsed through them. Nothing remotely familiar.

Most of the scratches looked like sticks crossed. One of the images appeared to be the head of a man with his hair straight up. It almost looked like a picture.

Theodore sat still for a moment. Picture?

It wasn't lettering he saw, it was pictographs. He scanned through the history of the last web pages he viewed. Two weeks earlier he'd read an article on bizarre news stories. One was about a scientist who claimed he'd found common ancient pictographs on six continents and claimed they were part of a prehistoric alphabet.

Theodore ran off the image of the alphabet. There was the image of the man with the prickly hair. It was supposed to represent the letter O.

He stared at the image of the scratches he'd hand drawn earlier. One with two sticks crossed at right angles was in the alphabet.

Theodore frantically matched up the seven letters.

They spelled bmocgew.

"Well, that doesn't make any sense," he groaned and stared at the scratches again in the picture. "Hang on. I think two of these letters aren't right." They were so close to some of the others, since each letter in the alphabet had two to four options. He substituted the letters. Still didn't make any sense. Theodore stared at the letters. What if the combinations were wrong? He began to write out all the various combinations of letters. Nothing came close to anything resembling anything. As he sat in frustration the phone rang; it was Roger. Theodore explained what he'd found and what he was doing. "Any ideas, Roger?"

"Describe the scratches to me."

"Well, they almost look Chinese, I guess."

"Didn't they read from back to front or left to right? Reverse them and see what we get," Roger said. "While I move to another part of the room, I'm getting static or some kind of buzzing on the phone."

"Why didn't I think of that?" Theodore did and still nothing made any sense, not until he came down to the first set of letters he'd been working on and changed the letter to another one he suspected it could be. "Oh. Fuck me."

"What? What's wrong?"

"They spell something alright. They spell 'WELCOME'."

As he said that Roger gasped into the cellphone. "That noise it's ... Oh my God, Hang on I'm going to turn off my cell and switch to movie mode. Call you right back."

"Roger, what, what the hell is going..."

The line went dead.

Tom opened his eyes. Samantha lay asleep beside him in his bed. He'd been glad to take the late flight out of LA and finally get back home yesterday. A sucker he'd been taken for a sucker, on the other hand if they could do that with him, what else could they generate? Hang on, this could be incredible, like that deck on the new StarTrek shows. What was it called, the HaloDeck, that's it!

The musky odor of sex hung in the air. She'd been great, as usual; that woman knew how to give great head. He couldn't sleep though, his head reeling coke. Its electric buzz still sending hunger into the part of him that should have been worn out and satisfied. God, I can't believe I'm still horny.

She didn't budge when he gave her a little push. You're out for the night and I'm laying here wide awake. Perhaps if I play with myself a little it'll help me to get some shuteye. He picked up the stack of 3D cards and flicked through them. He stopped and stared at one. I've never seen this one! Or have I?

A scene of a bed surrounded by canopy hung layers of white silk, and standing beside it a platinum blonde in a short blue teddy looking vaguely familiar. Where'd he seen her? The agent with the merchant's cards from the other day at the restaurant. What was her name?

"Sherida," the voice of the Hathor answered.

Tom jumped, he was in the card.

"I didn't know these cards could talk?"

"Didn't I tell you this second batch were far more advanced?" the Hathor replied.

"Yes." Something about this didn't seem quite right, seeing Sherida but hearing the Hathor's voice. Tom shrugged it off, all he could think of was what was hiding behind the curves of the silk teddy that clung to the hot blonde's body hiding enough to not see anything. Revealing enough to stir his imagination and want. The hunger from his loins, the hope where this was leading to.

Other moans filled the air. Tom looked around and realized there were other beds like this one, with couples making love. Men thrusting slowly into their women, women on top riding on their men's hardness. Lost in their passions, consumed by desire.

Sherida brought two glasses over to a stunned Tom and offered one to him. "Water to slake your thirst and clear the head, or perhaps some heady red wine. Or maybe you'd prefer what the one in the bed has to offer."

Tom pulled aside the veils and Samantha sat there naked on a bed of silk, rose petals spread all around. In her hands a silver platter with eight white lines. It was hard to concentrate, he wanted the hunger, the fire of the mind-blowing rush of the coke, the slip into oblivion. "No, I can't."

Something was wrong, no matter how advanced the cards were, there was no way Samantha should be here. It was like the cards were creating his deepest desires. Was this even possible?

"Come, instead, to us, my love." Other women slid past the veils of silk and entered the room. Tall voluptuous blondes, petite oriental ladies, and luscious ebony beauties.

"Let us give you pleasure, massage you." They held bowls of oils, smelling of patchouli and ylang ylang.

"No, I can't." But his erection was giving him away. The driving hardness, the fiery need to release from his building passions.

Two began to kiss each other. Shedding their clothes, hands fondling breasts with erect nipples, stroking each other between their legs. "Stay, watch us instead."

One of his strongest fantasies, most males. "I ... I ..."

Arousal began again. Two other women joined them and kneeled. They began to pleasure them with their tongues between the curls of softness.

Samantha snorted a line of coke into her nose and coughed. "Come on, have some, get high and stay just a little longer."

The two women threw their heads back and moaned as they pulled closer the two on their knees. Moans of other lovers ghosted through the room, calling to Tom to join them or watch.

"Yes, stay and let me do the same to you, as she does to me." The tall blonde pulled at the back of the head of the dark skinned girl licking at her. Sights of pink tongue darting through the dark triangle, shuddering as the throes of orgasm ran through her body.

Two other tall, lanky dark haired women entered and stood before him. Only as one got on her knees and pulled aside the silky veils of clothing did he realize they weren't truly women. "Or be with us." The one on her knees said as she/he sucked the other's hardness.

"Oh God." He'd been with a transsexual once on a dare, and swore he'd never do it again.

In his shock he dropped the card and sat up in bed.

Tom shook his head. "Man those new cards are unbelievable." Two lines of coke still remained on the bedside table. "Lord, do I need some to calm me down after that experience." Tom snorted the whiteness and choked. He remembered the night with the transsexual, had tried to forget about it. That night had shaken everything he'd believed in himself and his manhood. He'd enjoyed it too much.

He yawned, slipped back into the bed and brushed himself up against Samantha. His hands filling with the softness of her breasts. "No, this is all I really want right here. Grade A woman."

He dozed off holding her breasts and found himself back in the long hallway of lights; under each was a door. He stared at the numbered door beside him. It was his apartment, his current reality. Tom opened the door cautiously and stepped in. As he feared, there was no one there. His heart thumped. Why did he have to dream this again? Why? Because this is what he feared? Wasn't it?

A clunk of metal sounded from the living room and he went to investigate. The suit of armor stood there. Unable to stop himself he walked up to it and lifted the visor; it was empty. He breathed a sigh of relief and turned away, only to find another suit before him. No.

He ran for the door and bumped into another suit, which crashed to the floor, pieces falling every which way. The face-plate fell into his hands and he stared at the face, his own face, glaring up him, locked in the madness of ecstasy. NO.

He dropped the head-piece and ran from his room. He slammed the door and ran down the hallway. Other doors stood ajar, he slammed them as he ran by, at first, but there were so many he finally gave up and just ran. This is not what he wanted, he hated himself, his life. His aloneness. Tom ran faster, trying to reach the end of the hall, yet the lights only began to blur more quickly, never reaching the darkness at the end of hall. The blurs began to merge, he was stuck on a treadmill, one he couldn't escape. Finally they merged into one solid white light and, like the blast of a welder's torch, exploded into a million shards of light. All went mercifully black.

He opened his eyes and stood in the hallway again. "No, this is no good. Running doesn't help." He tried one of the doors and entered one of the rooms.

Ragged breathing, his, echoed from the darkness. The crack of a whip and searing pain. Searing exquisite pain. He opened his eyes. His body felt different, softer. He stared up at the blonde in the long black stiletto boots.

No. He was in the card of the two SM women.

Her whip lashed across his full breasts. Across tender nipples. No, this wasn't real, this was a dream, but try as hard as he could he couldn't wake up. Every time he opened his eyes, he was her. Tied, submitting, enduring, no enjoying the pain he'd subjected himself to.

Tom screamed at the renewed crack of the whip.

The blonde knew what she was doing, she was obviously an expert dominatrix. Just enough not to draw blood, just to arouse.

He felt the moistness flowing from him, the need to release growing. Mixing with the pain, pain triggering pleasure.

He closed his eyes and stood in the hallway again. Tom took a few more steps and entered the next room.

"No", he cried, arms bound to the bed. He was now in the card of the man tied to the bed with the redhead. Hot candle wax dripped on him. He screamed again, tried to speak, but couldn't. He had no voice. Everything was beginning to get too blurry, too hard to focus, to know what to do. He closed his eyes and stood out in the hallway again.

"No, this is madness."

The door before him opened and he fell into the room. A whip sang across his backside, across his buttocks. Leather clung to his body, held his wrists to the wall. A rough man's hand pinched his nipple. No, not this, not the scene of the two men.

Then before his eyes he saw the tip of a black leather boot presented for him. Like the dutiful slave he was, his bright red lipstick smeared the boot as he kissed it, licking again and again.

Another crack of the whip, flooding his wetness, increasing the need for release. His only goal, though, was to pleasure; he himself was denied the same. To reward his mistress. He dared a glance upward and spied the dark triangle before him. His goal, to part those pubic hairs and give pleasure to that darkness that owned him. As his painted lips drew closer he caught the sight of the hardness growing from the center of the darkness. "No, God, no."

A gloved hand on the back of his head drew him in. His mouth opened, he couldn't stop himself from doing what he desired the most and began to suck greedily. Another she-male entered the room and pulled garments aside. His eyes opened in shock at the size of her hard-on. He tried to pull away, to scream, but couldn't as the hand on back of his head kept him skewered in place. He looked up and saw himself leering down at himself, white stains around his red inflamed nose. The second one thrust herself into him. "NO!"

The darkness swallowed him, frightening him. "No," he cried, as inky blackness poured all around him.

Tom finally managed to wrestle himself back to consciousness. Jesus, he thought, the cards were taking over his dreams, like a computer virus. Samantha hadn't budged. Tom got out of bed and staggered to the bathroom, opened the door, and stared at the image of one woman binding another to the white porcelain god before him. "No!" he screamed. He closed the door and reopened it. Only the white throne stared back.

Nuts! He was going crazy. Either he had taken too much coke or was still in the illusion of the cards. Maybe they were getting stronger, taking over. Transcending the boundaries of the cards. That's it! The whole floor was a card somehow.

If the two women could just suddenly appear in his washroom, then they definitely could project the illusion of a security guard, a whole floor, or even — damn it — a whole building. Crap. He'd been sucked in for sure.

Tom washed his face and stared into the mirror. The reflection showed a hilltop in the background. Tom looked behind him, but just the shower stall stared back.

Moans, he heard moans. In the mirror, himself bound on his knees before his she-male mistress, pleasuring her with his mouth. Only she was him, painted face and all, and he was rewarding her like a good slave should. Her gloved hand holding his head in place. The realization hit, that's exactly what he was, slave to his own desires and himself.

NO, Tom jerked back. I like being sexual and aroused. Only not like this, was this where I was heading? Down some kinky perversion into stranger and stranger weirdo crap?

Only this hadn't happened before, this wasn't a continuation of the card, but another scene that hadn't existed in any of them. His internal arousal tore at him. I have to overcome this, only I don't want to.

He fell back against the plastic of the shower curtain and into the tub. Instead of hard porcelain slamming into his spinning head, Tom fell against the sand of a beach. Beach? What's happened? He closed his eyes again and when he opened them he was back in the shower stall.

Maybe he was still dreaming, running from himself. He reached for the showerhead and cranked on the water. Stars, planets, the dark matter of the cosmos poured out, drowning him, losing him in the dark empty eternity of space. Sucked into the vast emptiness filling the bathtub.

The stack of holographic cards in the next room fluttered to the ground as the shower ran continuing to run its stream into the now empty stall.

The Hathor stooped to shut off the shower tap. He went to the next room to retrieve the cards and tore them into pieces. With a click of his fingers they vanished. He looked around the otherwise empty suite to make sure nothing of what was attempted remained. So many attempt, so few succeed.

Somewhere in the darkness of space a voice cried out before it was locked in the bitter frigid cold for eternity.

"Shit, double shit." Theodore stood stunned with the silence of the cellphone in his ear. He glanced at the number and redialed; busy. He thought a moment. Crap, I can't stand it. Need to find out what happened.

Theodore grabbed his car keys and ran to the front of his home as his phone notified him of an incoming text.

"You ain't going to believe this"

Theodore stopped at his front door, one foot with shoe on and rang Roger. "What's up? What happened? You okay?"

"I'm uploading the movie I just took and sending it to your phone. This started to happen just as we were talking. Then all hell broke loose as you told me of the word the scratches formed."

"All hell? What happened, for God's sake just tell me." The line went dead.

Theodore gritted his teeth as stood there waiting impatiently for the critical seconds that the internet cloud took to resend the movie from Roger to him.

He clicked on the movie that Roger had just recorded for him moments earlier. He watched the minute or so long movie clip twice before calling his friend. This just wasn't possible.

"Did I just see what you just sent me?"

"Yup, the second you said 'Welcome' to me. Just before that happened I walked over to the alien metal because I could hear something in the room. A humming, growing louder. It never dawned on me that it could be coming from the alien object.

I thought I was hearing things, maybe background static from the cellphones, you know. Bad reception sometimes. The humming began to get louder as you were deciphering the letters. When you uttered 'Welcome' it stopped and began to glow from a dull blue to orange to red to white, brilliant white and like I videoed it…"

"Vanished." They both uttered.

"I'm coming over." Roger jumped in his car and drove as slow as he could, wanting to drive like a madman, but knowing that accidents are more than possible, along with less than understanding police officers. How could he explain that to anyone?

Theodore stared at the room, the empty table with not even an ash on it to tell what had been there before. "It has completely vanished. How?"

"Don't know, but we done it."

"Only what have we done?"

Theodore scratched his head. "Well that's the deeper question. There's no news of anything weird or spiritual on any of my Facebook accounts or Twitter feeds. I put out questions asking if anyone felt or saw anything. No reports of any light trails leaving the Earth. Nothing in the media. It's like whatever that hunk of metal was, has completely vanished and whatever was out there to congratulate us isn't there."

"Well we both know that, or assume from our memories, that it was put into us by my angel."

"Or some kind of alien being?"

"You'd think Buddha or some enlightened being would show up and ask us out for a couple of beers to chat or something."

"That would be cool."

"Only he didn't."

"Think we're too late? I mean as a species. Everything I've read indicates we should have broken out of our mindsets centuries ago."

"But that brings me back to the question. Why would your angel have just planted them in us? Doesn't make any sense. Except I guess we just have to accept we did it, did something and wait."

"How long?"

"Don't know could be a lifetime? I mean the next solar system with possible life bearing planet we currently know is a rocky planet discovered circling Proxima Centauri twelve light years away. 39,000k per hour is the fastest a NASA shuttle can travel. To travel one light year. Radio waves travel at the speed of light, 300,000 K's per second. So even if we could send out a radio wave signal from this planet or this metal object, which has now vanished or possibly been converted into a radio signal it would take at least twelve years to reach the nearest possible life supporting world. So it would take…"

"A long time I get it. Oh, I like the idea of having Buddha show up and meet us in the pub."

"I'll bet he's got some stories to tell."

"Yeah and a wicked sense of humor."

Circling Saturn, the Moon of Titan suddenly shifted from a blue light spectrum into a subtle green.

"Damn," rasped a reptilian voice.

If you really enjoyed this Novel,
Please, feel free to leave a review

The author will highly appreciate it
Thank You!

AFTERWORD

Other Novels by Frank Talaber
Stillwater Runs Deep Series

Book One: Raven's Lament
(based on a true incident)

A madman cuts down a rare tree in protest of logging, releasing something he didn't intend to. Reporter Brooke Grant investigates the story, finds the love of his life, only to lose her to said being. Enlisting the aid of a deranged shaman he has to save his love and stop the world from being changed forever.

Reviews

This novel has the ring of an epic "Lord of the Rings" journey -this is one journey that I'll always remember!

Stephanie A. Bridgeman/ The Glow Faeries

This is one of these books that you don't want to lay down until it's finished. Great stuff!

Tara Swanson

"After being stranded twenty kilometers from the nearest road at the tip of Rose Spit, Haida Gwaii, and having to push Frank's spanking new SUV a few kilometers along the beach before the tide came in and we ran out of booze, my first reaction on being asked to write a back cover blurb was, "over my dead body." Some people will do anything to get an endorsement."

Susan Musgrave/Cargo of Orchids/Given

On the west Coast, a journalist investigates a killing linked to destruction of old growth forest on First Nations land, and finds a spirit war as well as a real-work environmental struggle. He also finds love and meaning. It's a lovely, timely story line, and the outcome is arrived at in a surprising confluence of plot and subplot which makes the book ultimately charming and moving.

Candas Jane Dorsey

Book Two: The Lure

Ever go out drinking and don't remember what you did? What if there was a bar where spirits use your body for whatever they want until you sober up? What if the city's mayor has been murdered, his family missing, no clues and a witch has been released from her centuries old imprisonment? A deranged shaman shows up leaving clues and vanishes. So begins police detective, Carol Ainsworth's first big case.

Reviews

Your book kept my attention riveted from beginning to end. I liked the way you presented the female character being in control of the outcome and the fact the story was based on local settings. i.e. Victoria, B.C. Canada Riveting Work .....

Linda Low

A refreshing change from the usual and all too familiar cast of deities and spirits. Talaber pulls his characters from the vast and untapped riches of aboriginal myth and legend, bringing to life their intricate stories largely unfamiliar to wider audiences. He intertwines their ancient tales with the dark, gritty and dangerous under belly of contemporary urban life. The whole makes for an interesting and compelling read with an ending that's impossible to predict.

Robert Winslow

Damn Frank — this writing is as tactile as a 1955 T-Bird. Very nice descriptions, good dialogue, a thinking man's book but one that can be read entirely for pleasure. Good work.

Michael Arkin/Judicial Indiscretion

Paranormal fantasy, mystery thriller rolled into one. The Lure is a well-crafted story that builds suspense through flowing narrative, life-like characters, and believable dialogue. If you're a fan of any of the above mentioned genres, or if you're just looking for a page turner to get lost in, The Lure will not disappoint.

Cris Pasqueralle/Destiny Revealed

A gritty book flavored with primitive urges and mysticism. As I followed Carol's foray into the realm of shamanism, I realized that it took a special touch to pull off a complicated plot the way you did. Your prose was concise, powerfully descriptive, the dialogue lively, and your photographic mastery of the fixtures and streets in Vancouver's hub, in clear evidence.

Kenneth Edward Lim/The North Korean

Carol, the head detective, has to solve several murder cases: with many twists and turns. There's Shamans, Animal Spirits, and "The Lure" thrown in for good measure. No wonder, Carol wanted to resign! Yes, this novel is a roller-coaster ride, with the author cleverly hinting along the way, ending with a roller coaster ride! Read this book. It is different. It's as if Elmore Leonard has risen as a shaman, to guide others to write about Indian lore.

Nancy Bridgeman

Your book was a rollercoaster ride thorough my emotions which, when I got off, left me stunned and breathless.

Your portrayal of sociopaths and the criminal mind in the pursuit of the sexually willing was so disturbing I had nightmares and had to set the novel aside for days. But the writing was so compelling I had to finish it, and I'm glad I persevered.

I literally cheered "go get them!" when Charlie used his protectors to deal rather uniquely with the antagonists.

I was enlightened to the Native spiritual culture which pleased me for which I now have a greater understanding and respect.

Carol G.

Book Three: The Awakening

Its Ghostbusters teamed up with a female Mickey Spillane who has a Native Shaman sidekick nuttier than a squirrels winter stash as a side kick.

Agatha Christie, roll over in your grave, new sleuths on the prowl. A deranged shaman breaks his way into jail to stop all hell from breaking free while police detective Carol Ainsworth has to bring justice to a forest being's murdered mother.

How angry would a mythical god be if he found himself beginning to awake inside a mortal after centuries? The duo are determined to find out who killed the previous native elder before all lightning and thunder breaks loose. They encounter deranged inmates, mystical beings, ancient serpents, wood sprites and someone who should have been dead long ago.

Not your usual crime/mystery!

Not your usual criminal investigators!

You thought Jack Nicholson was mad in The Shining...

Wait until you meet Charlie Stillwaters in the Sweat lodge.

Reviews

There are many aspects true to First Nation's beliefs. For example the transformation of animals and anomalies within our realm. Frank Talaber's writing is clear and concise, leaving no grey areas. But his true talent as a writer is not only a sense of time, history and capturing First Nation's humor, but going from the real to the surreal and the supernatural. A gift he plies very well.

Tom Patterson Nuu-Cha-Nulth Artist and Master Carver

Just when I was beginning to wonder where the next great Canadian story teller would emerge from, Frank Talaber has written a modern crime mystery with a twist. In "The Awakening" Talaber weaves the richness of Canada's west coast aboriginal spirituality into the science of modern forensics. CSI comes to Haida Gwaii as the shaman and the detective conduct an investigation that will take them and the reader on a journey to a place where murder, redemption and ancient mysticism intersect.

Michael G. de Jong, QC, Minister of Finance, Government House Leader,

Province of British Columbia

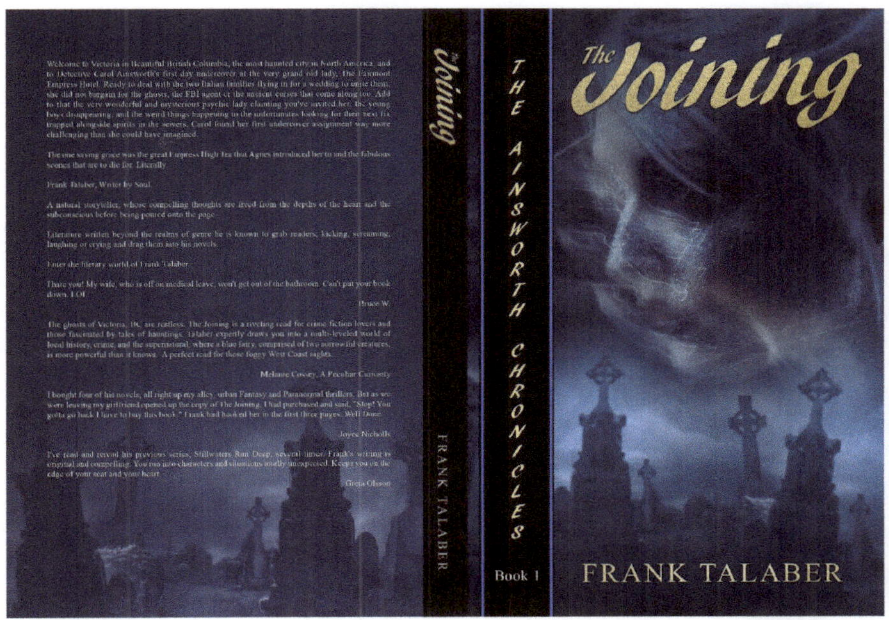

The Ainsworth Chronicles,
Book One: The Joining

Welcome to Victoria in Beautiful British Columbia, the most haunted city in North America, and to Detective Carol Ainsworth's first day undercover at the very grand old lady, The Fairmont Empress Hotel. Ready to deal with the two Italian families flying in for a wedding to unite them, she did not bargain for the ghosts, the FBI agent or the ancient curses that come along too. Add to that the very wonderful and mysterious psychic lady claiming you've invited her, the young boys disappearing, and the weird things happening to the unfortunates looking for their next fix trapped alongside spirits in the sewers, Carol found her first undercover assignment way more challenging than she could have imagined.

The one saving grace was the great Empress High Tea that Agnes introduced her to and the fabulous scones that are to die for. Literally.

Reviews

I hate you! My wife, who is off on medical leave, won't get out of the bathroom. Can't put your book down. LOL.

Bruce W.

The ghosts of Victoria, BC are restless. The Joining is a riveting read for crime fiction lovers and those fascinated by tales of hauntings. Talaber expertly draws you into a multi-leveled world of local history, crime, and the supernatural, where a blue fairy, comprised of two sorrowful creatures, is more powerful than it knows. A perfect read for those foggy West Coast nights.

Melanie Cossey, A Peculiar Curiosity

I bought four of his novels, all right up my alley, urban Fantasy and Paranormal thrillers. But as we were leaving my girlfriend opened up the copy of The Joining, I had purchased and said, "Stop! You gotta go back I have to buy this book." Frank had hooked her in the first three pages. Well Done.

Joyce Nicholls

I've read and reread his previous series, Stillwaters Run Deep, several times. Frank's writing is original and compelling. You run into characters and situations totally unexpected. Keeps you on the edge of your seat and your heart.

Greta Olsson

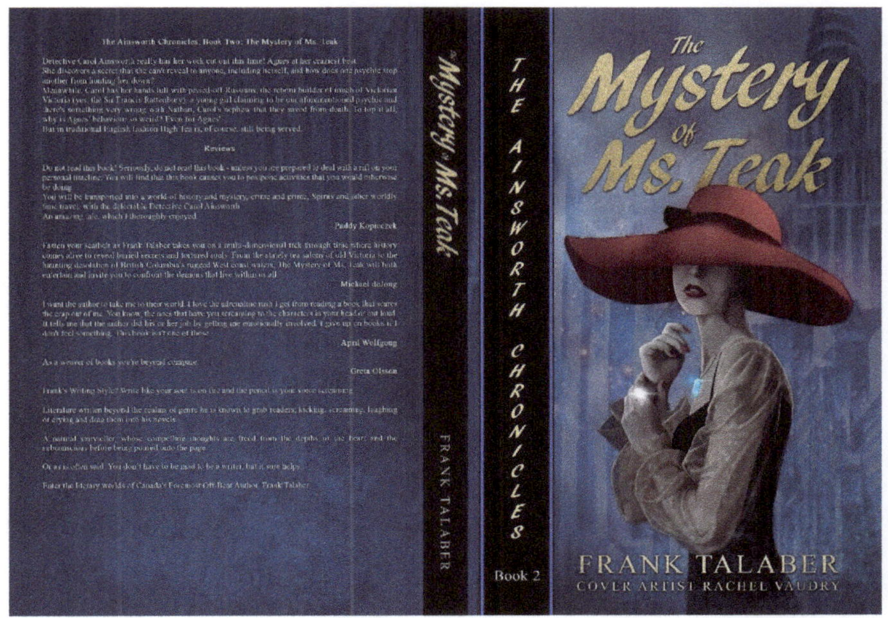

The Ainsworth Chronicles, Book Two: The Mystery of Ms. Teak

Agnes at her craziest best. Only what secret does she have to hide from herself and the one she thought dead? How does one psychic stop another from hunting her down, especially when the other hires the services of a mystical being long thought perished! As for Carol, she has her hands full with pissed-off Russians, the reborn builder of much of Victorian Victoria (yes, the Sir Francis Rattenbury), a young girl claiming to be our aforementioned psychic, and, to top it all off, there's something very wrong with Nathan, her nephew that they saved from death. But in traditional English fashion High Tea is of course still being served.

Reviews

Do not read this book! Seriously, do not read this book — unless you are prepared to deal with a rift on your personal timeline. You will find that this book causes you to postpone activities that you would otherwise be doing. You will be transported into a world of history and mystery, crime and grime, Spirits and other worldly time travel, with the delectable Detective Carol Ainsworth. An amazing tale, which I thoroughly enjoyed.

Paddy Kopieczek

Fasten your seatbelt as Frank Talaber takes you on a multi-dimensional trek through time where history comes alive to reveal buried secrets and tortured souls. From the stately tea salons of old Victoria to the haunting desolation of British Columbia's rugged West coast waters, The Mystery of Ms. Teak will both entertain and invite you to confront the demons that live within us all.

Michael deJong

I want the author to take me to their world. I love the adrenaline rush I get from reading a book that scares the crap out of me. You know, the ones that have you screaming to the characters in your head or out loud. It tells me that the author did his or her job by getting me emotionally involved. I give up on books if I don't feel something. This book isn't one of those.

April Wolfgong

As a weaver of books you're beyond compare.

Greta Olsson

FRANK'S BIO

Frank Talaber was born in Beaverlodge, Alberta, where the claim to fame is a fox with flashing eyes in the only pub. Yeah, big place, that's why his family left when he was knee high to a grasshopper and moved to Edmonton, Alberta. Eventually he got tired of ten months of winter and two of bad slush and moved to Chilliwack, BC. Great place, Cedar trees, can cut the grass nine months of the year and, oh, it does snow here once or twice. Just enough to have to find out what happened to the bloody snow shovel and have to use it. GRRR.

He's spent most of his life either fixing cars or managing automotive shops and is a licensed automotive technician. However, it's the little muses that keep twigging on his pencil won't let his writing pad stay blank.

He has several novels published, which include the genres of urban fantasy, thriller, crime and romance. He also has written in science fiction, spiritual, erotica and comedy genres.

When asked once, "where does this creativity spring from?" he answered, "It's the Gypsy blood from my mother's Hungarian ancestry."

Literary madness that drives his wife crazy when he leaves their bed in the middle of the night to pound out some sort of prosaic induced brilliance. "Here we go again, the next War and Peace, Aka 21st century," she moans, only to realize it's either gibberish or there's no lead in his pencil and he's scribbled on sixteen blank pages in the dark.

When asked about Frank Talaber's Writing Style? He usually responds with: Mix Dan Millman (Way of The Peaceful Warrior) with Charles De Lint (Moonheart) and throw in a mad scattering of Tom Robbins (Even Cowgirls Get The Blues).

PS: He's better looking than Stephen King (Carrie, The Stand, It, The Shining) and his romantic stuff will have you gasping quicker than Robert James Waller (Bridges Of Madison County).

Visit Frank Talaber's Published Author page on Facebook at:

https://www.facebook.com/FrankTalaber/

(If you want to join his fans' newsletter to hear about his latest ventures, go to the above page and scroll down on the column on the left).

Website:

https://franktalaberpublishedauthor.wordpress.com/

Facebook Short Stories Page:

https://www.facebook.com/ franktalaberpublishedauthor/

Twitter:

@FrankTalaber https://about.me/ftalaber

Linkedin:

https://www.linkedin.com/feed/

Then search for my name.